"No man gives me orders, my lord," Claudia said.

Lord Hawke drew in a deep breath. "By heavens, you need someone to tame you, madam."

"Truly? Well, it won't be you!" With that, she backed up to the garden gate, fumbled until she found the latch, then opened it. Her intent to escape her tormentor was foiled when he crossed the few steps now separating them.

He stood at her side, examining her. "What makes you fight me?"

"Fight, sir? I fight with no one. I am a peace-loving woman. Surely you make more from our words than is warranted?"

He firmed his lips, then took a step that brought him up against her. "So you love peace? What else do you love, widow?" His voice had dropped to a low growl, like that of a predatory cat.

"My privacy." She licked her suddenly dry lips, wondering how to deal with this man. Her pulse galloped madly. He was a menace to her hard-won tranquillity.

Without warning, he dipped his head and kissed her.

More praise for
Emily Hendrickson

"Emily Hendrickson's knack for imbuing her characters with realistic foibles assures us that they're always instantly sympathetic." —*Romantic Times*

"When Ms. Hendrickson's name is on the cover, you know you'll be satisfied." —Romance Reviews Today

My Lady Faire

Emily Hendrickson

A SIGNET BOOK

SIGNET
Published by New American Library, a division of
Penguin Group (USA) Inc., 375 Hudson Street,
New York, New York 10014, USA
Penguin Group (Canada), 10 Alcorn Avenue, Toronto,
Ontario M4V 3B2, Canada (a division of Pearson Penguin Canada Inc.)
Penguin Books Ltd., 80 Strand, London WC2R 0RL, England
Penguin Ireland, 25 St. Stephen's Green, Dublin 2,
Ireland (a division of Penguin Books Ltd.)
Penguin Group (Australia), 250 Camberwell Road, Camberwell, Victoria 3124,
Australia (a division of Pearson Australia Group Pty. Ltd.)
Penguin Books India Pvt. Ltd., 11 Community Centre, Panchsheel Park,
New Delhi - 110 017, India
Penguin Group (NZ), cnr Airborne and Rosedale Roads, Albany,
Auckland 1310, New Zealand (a division of Pearson New Zealand Ltd.)
Penguin Books (South Africa) (Pty.) Ltd., 24 Sturdee Avenue,
Rosebank, Johannesburg 2196, South Africa

Penguin Books Ltd., Registered Offices:
80 Strand, London WC2R 0RL, England

First published by Signet, an imprint of New American Library,
a division of Penguin Group (USA) Inc.

First Printing, March 2005
10 9 8 7 6 5 4 3 2 1

PUBLISHER'S NOTE
This is a work of fiction. Names, characters, places, and incidents either are
the product of the author's imagination or are used fictitiously, and any resemblance to actual persons, living or dead, business establishments, events, or
locales is entirely coincidental.

I dedicate this book to my dear husband, John, who has supported me in my writing career.
And with kind thoughts
to those who have encouraged me over the years—
my daughter, Kirsten, and sisters, Irene and Evelyn.

As well, a special note of thanks to Sherrie Holmes, for all she has done.

Chapter One

August 1817

"***M****ark my words, he is a dangerous man, my dear, and never forget it! And he has come home!*"

An ominous roll of thunder crashed through the house following the sharp spear of blue-white lightning that lit up the dull gray afternoon. The nicely plump woman who had been standing by the large window hastily moved away as though afraid she might be struck. Her auburn curls were in slight disarray as she smoothed the front of her dress in some agitation. She turned to face the other occupant of the room—the slim blonde seated neatly at a small desk, a pencil in hand and wearing an expression of patience.

Claudia, Lady Fairfax, put aside the drawing on which she had been working to tilt her head in a considering way. "He does not frighten me in the least. Come, Olivia, what can he do? Granted, he is Edward's other guardian, but he hasn't been in the area for over a year. Why should he bother us now?"

"Your year of mourning is up—that is why." Olivia Greene stared with concerned eyes at her benefactress and cousin by marriage. "I am not the least surprised that he returned from London . . . or wherever he has been." She implied all manner of wicked things in the tone she used, to Claudia's amusement.

Claudia left her small desk, placing a sheet of paper over her drawings to protect them from smudging. She straightened the pillows on the sofa before seating herself in anticipation of tea.

Olivia joined Claudia on the sofa, looking as though she wanted to continue her dire predictions.

"What utter nonsense! That is too silly for words." Claudia thought she sounded quite brave and matter-of-fact. However, inwardly she trembled just a trifle. *That man,* as she had thought of him, was too like a hawk about to swoop down on her innocent head. Without conscious thought, she reached up to adjust the confection of lace and cambric that perched on her blond curls. Olivia scolded that she was too young for a matron's cap. At twenty-seven Claudia felt ancient. Perhaps small boys did that to one. The sound of steps thumping down the stairs presaged the arrival of her stepson.

"Mama," Edward cried as he dashed into the sitting room where the ladies of the house preferred to gather, "did you hear that thunder? It was ferocious!"

Claudia gathered the seven-year-old boy to her side. She smiled at her stepson before bestowing a hug around his slim, restless person. "Indeed, I did. I thought it rather awesome." If his hug was a trifle anxious, she gave no indication of it. "It isn't anything to worry about."

"Do you suppose Lord Hawke heard it too?" The boy gazed up at her with a shrewd expression on his face.

"I imagine he did. He lives not too far from here, as you know." Claudia guessed what was to follow.

"Perhaps he will come to cheer us up. This is a very gray day and I am tired of my toys." He gave his stepmother an ingenuous smile. "He always brings me something fun."

"Edward," Claudia cautioned after a glance at Olivia, "we do not like people merely because they bring us things."

"But he does, and I do like him. He is my other guardian," the boy added with irrefutable logic.

There was no argument to this line, for indeed, Noel Clifford, Lord Hawke, their wealthy, handsome, intimidating, and infuriating neighbor, had been named as the coguardian for Edward, now the young Lord Fairfax, when his father had been killed. That he had in the past brought clever toys to amuse his ward could not be denied. And that Edward had longed for his presence this past year could also not be disputed. Only Claudia, and perhaps the peace-loving Olivia, did not wish him to visit the Fairfax home.

It wasn't that Claudia regretted the death of the previous Lord Fairfax. She had been relieved that she no longer had to deal with her much older and very wayward husband. But he had been a barrier of sorts against the world.

"True, dearest. But you must be aware that Lord Hawke is a very busy gentleman and you cannot expect him to call on us when he has barely come home. Perhaps in a few days he may come." She wondered if she could count on such a thought. She was well aware that his lordship would do whatever he pleased. He was not one to abide by conventions. He skirted impropriety by the simple fact of his wealth and handsome visage. Ironic, how a man might do the indecorous with impunity. If she dared to step a foot beyond what was fitting, she would have the wrath of all the local gossips on her head within minutes.

Mrs. Tibbins, her stalwart housekeeper, marched into the room. The prim expression on her face told Claudia that she was about to receive some unpleasant news.

"Lord Hawke is here, madam. I expect you will wish to see him?" Her tone indicated she knew that her mistress had little choice but to invite his lordship into the sitting room.

She dared not refuse him, and the sitting room was their most pleasant room on a rainy day, with a fire burning merrily in the grate and two Argand lamps to take away from the gloom. It would be disagreeable to move to the more formal and only slightly warmed drawing room. While the weather was not as chilly as it had been the previous August, the house felt dampish during a rainstorm.

"Best bring tea and cakes," Claudia said, troubled at this invasion of his hawkish lordship.

"Tea," said the gentleman in question, following on Mrs. Tibbins's heels. His voice sounded very satisfied. The deep, rich tone always sent a tremor up Claudia's spine. She had fought the effect he had on her, but his lazy regard did not make it easy for her. "What better way to spend a rainy afternoon." He strolled into the room, quite at ease in the Fairfax residence. Indeed, when the previous Lord Fairfax had been alive, Lord Hawke had been here often. He followed the housekeeper into the sitting room, certain of his welcome in his ward's home.

Claudia hastily rose, bowed just enough to be proper, then gestured for her guest to be seated. How good it was that Olivia remained to serve as a buffer. Edward was hardly chaperon enough for a man admittedly handsome and too impressive for Claudia's peace of mind.

"I vow I am surprised to see you out and about on such a day as this." She glanced at the view beyond her window where rain still streamed down the panes, although it had lessened some. The thunder had faded to a mere rumble and no more lightning stabbed the earth below.

"A little wet never hurt anyone. I thought to see how Edward is getting along. I knew he would be indoors on such a day, so likely to be available for a chat." His gaze settled on Claudia as though he knew how he affected her and how reluctant she was to have him here. No matter that he unsettled her, he generally sent Edward into transports of delight that were hard to contain. His lordship quirked a brow at her stare.

Claudia collected her wits, nodding in agreement. "True, true. I would not wish him to catch a cold in the rain. You never know what might develop."

A lazy smile lit up his eyes before he dropped his gaze to his ward. "And you, my boy, are you preparing to head off to Eton this autumn?"

Edward looked to his mother. "I do not think so, sir. Mama said I have plenty of time before I need leave here for school."

"Is that so?" Lord Hawke pinned Claudia with a cold look that was almost tangible.

The three words struck dread in her heart. Even though Edward was not her own son, she loved him as dearly as though he was born of her body. She had heard too many things about the difficulties for boys at Eton. She wanted Edward to be a little older, better able to defend himself against the bullies likely to pick on him. He was slender, almost feminine with his auburn curls and wide brown eyes, and a dreamer—just the sort of boy most apt to be a target of nasty teasing.

"Olivia and I teach him, with the vicar giving him lessons in Latin. Edward is doing very well right here at home." She hated the defensive note in her voice. *She* was the properest judge of what was right for the boy. What did a bachelor know about raising children, pray tell?

"The vicar? Hmm. That is the new chap recently installed, is it not? The handsome fellow with the red curls and languishing looks that the village maids sigh over?"

"True, the vicar is new, but appears to be well taught. Edward likes him very well." Claudia prayed her son would not add any comments on the subject.

"He likes Mama. I heard Mrs. Tibbins say so." Edward gave a satisfied sigh. "Everyone likes Mama, 'specially her fine blue eyes."

"Another one of Mrs. Tibbins's sayings?" The viscount lounged back in his chair, very much at his ease while he cast measuring glances at Claudia.

No reply was given as the housekeeper bustled into the room with a large tea tray complete with all needed for a splendid afternoon tea. Betsy followed with a tray that held a bounty of delights: scones, seed cake, plum cake, and slivers of sandwiches in the event the earl was hungry. Edward eyed the latter with a hungry gaze.

"How any child can eat as much as that boy and still stay as slim as a reed I do not know," Olivia said with a smile after accepting a steaming cup of tea. Her own plump self was evidence that she struggled with her desire for scones and cake.

"He dashes up and down the stairs and heaven knows what else," Claudia said, smiling fondly at the lad.

"He should be going off to school to join other boys his age. There is more to being at Eton than education, you know. He has to learn how to get along in this world. Plus he would be given a wider exposure to what he needs to know." Hawke cast her a look that dared her to disagree with him.

Claudia steeled herself to resist his arguments, for she was well aware they had merit. "In due time. His father wished him to attend Eton, and provision has been made for that day. I believe he still has much to learn first that we are able to teach him. My father, the Reverend Herbert, coached boys going to Eton until they were ready. Edward is not ready."

"Edward," the viscount said abruptly, "there is a

package in the entry hall for you. I think it is something you will enjoy." He watched while the lad bowed and expressed his thanks before dashing from the room following a glance at his mother to see if she approved.

"That is most kind of you, Lord Hawke," Claudia said with formality masking her feelings regarding his gifts. "But please do not think you must bring Edward something each time you come. He has a great many toys as it is."

"You restrict the boy." He dismissed the notion that Edward didn't need more toys with a wave of his hand. "He needs a man's influence in his life." His voice sounded harsh. He *looked* harsh in the delicate environs of the feminine sitting room, decorated in cream and rose. He was like a hawk in a bed of pansies about to pounce on a wayward mouse.

Claudia barely refrained from a shiver at the intensity of his gaze on her. She had forgotten the intense blue of his eyes. They seemed to see to her very heart. At her side Olivia sputtered a denial totally ignored by the infuriating man.

"I admit it is difficult without his father here. Not that his father was around all that much," Claudia added reflectively. "I still say Edward needs another year or two before he goes off to the hazards of Eton."

Olivia sought to ease the tension by offering the plate of sandwiches. The viscount took the entire plate, setting it on the small table at his side while he proceeded to demolish one after another. He glanced up to catch Claudia's wide-eyed look, then laughed.

"I haven't eaten since breaking my fast early this morning. What a good thing it is that Mrs. Tibbins hasn't forgotten what a man needs."

Claudia's mouth went dry at his expression. She was not an untutored spinster, although her husband had visited her bed rarely once he decided she wouldn't bear him a second son. Still, she could read desire in that look. She would have to be on her guard from now on. As Olivia had pointed out, the year of mourning was up.

"Mama! Mama! Look what Lord Hawke brought me!" Edward cried, dragging a large rocking horse into the room. It was gaily painted and irresistible to any child.

Claudia leaped to her feet to help. The thing was almost larger than Edward. She gave his lordship a flashing look, then shook her head in dismay.

"See, Mama! I can ride it!" The slender child clambered onto the large wooden steed to pick up the reins in a most masterly fashion. Then he rocked back and forth with great determination.

"Indeed, love, I can see you will be a topping horseman."

"He has his own pony, does he not?" Lord Hawke had set aside the now-empty plate to join Claudia by the rocking horse. His words were innocent enough if you didn't pick up on the challenge in them.

"Ah, no, he does not. There isn't a horse in the stable that is proper for a lad his age. I haven't sought a pony for him." Oh, how she hated to admit her delay in obtaining a pony. Somehow, after her husband's death while coming home from the village she couldn't manage it. The accident was the result of a shying horse toppling the carriage. Lord Fairfax had died instantly. The thought of Edward on even a pony was abhorrent.

"I shall take care of it for you."

Claudia turned to look at her nemesis. All she could see in his eyes was sympathy. He knew nothing of her personal life with her husband. Perhaps Hawke thought she pined for Fairfax, mourned his passing. Well, in a way she did, but not in any romantic manner. It was like missing the flu once it's over. You were thankful for its departure.

"Indeed, that is not necessary, Lord Hawke. I can have Jem Groom locate a suitable mount for Edward. He has a way with horses and knows what is available locally." Claudia licked her suddenly dry lips. The man next to her exuded power, a force that swept all in his wake. She was determined not to succumb to any blandishment he might offer in any way.

"We shall see. I'll have a chat with Jem."

Claudia firmed her lips lest she say something ill-advised. This man rattled her to the point of rashness on her part. "Yes, I imagine you would do that regardless of what I might say—or object. It is not necessary for you to interfere in our lives, Lord Hawke." If only she might persuade him of that; the peace would be so lovely.

He bestowed a lazy grin on her that made her pulse gallop. "Someday," he said very quietly, "I shall hear you say my name. Somehow, I believe Noel would sound very sweet on your lips." He quirked a brow as though he knew how this sort of teasing upset her. His gaze settled on her lips, and she swore she could almost feel his burning touch on them.

"It would be most improper, my lord." Claudia was determined to be demure and amiable, even if it killed her.

"Well, that is a handsome gift, Lord Hawke," Olivia inserted into the thickened atmosphere. She left the sofa to admire Edward's latest acquisition. Casting a shy glance at Claudia, she added, "You will need a strong man to carry the rocking horse up to Edward's room."

With great haste, Claudia replied, "He can have it here for a time. Then we can admire his horsemanship."

"Coward," Lord Hawke murmured just loud enough for her to hear him.

"Not in the least. I shall derive great pleasure from watching him," she insisted.

Lord Hawke failed to respond to this. He glanced at the neat stack of papers on her little desk close to where he stood. Without asking permission, he shifted the top paper aside.

"Still drawing flowers, are you? Delightful work, my dear."

Claudia longed to scream at him to go away, leave her alone, and stop harassing her with his veiled remarks and cunning looks.

From his perch atop his new wooden horse Edward thought to add to the conversation. "Mama draws fairies, too. She sees them at the bottom of our garden." He nodded for emphasis before resuming his determined rocking.

Claudia suspected her cheeks burned. "One does entertain with fairy stories, you know." She did see the fairies, but thought it prudent not to reveal the fact. Hawke might have her declared incompetent to care for Edward.

"Do they have happy endings?" he asked, the threat of a laugh lingering in his voice.

"All Mama's stories have happy endings," Edward replied on her behalf, evidently deciding he was well equipped to answer any questions dealing with fairy tales.

Olivia turned to face the enemy. "She paints flowers on china, and soon she plans to paint the fairies as well."

"Ah, she will be 'my lady faire'—is that it?"

"Such nonsense," Claudia sputtered. "I enjoy my painting. And if I add a fairy now and again to amuse my son what is there to it?" She tilted her chin, giving him a challenging look.

"More tea, anyone?" Olivia urged.

"By all means," the viscount replied, guiding Claudia back to the sofa and this time seating himself at her side, much to her discomfiture.

Olivia poured each of them another cup of tea. Mrs.

Tibbins appeared at the doorway, that prim look fixed to her face once more. "The vicar, ma'am."

"Show him in, by all means, Mrs. Tibbins."

The housekeeper nodded, looking like a satisfied cat.

Within minutes the young vicar arrived, his red hair tousled and the languishing looks Lord Hawke had mentioned in evidence. "Good afternoon. I have come to see how Edward is doing with his lessons." He turned his attention from Claudia to the man seated next to her, narrowing his eyes a trifle as he did. "Good day to you, Lord Hawke. How pleasant to see you once again."

"The attractions of London pall after a time. There is much to be said about the charms of the country." He sounded amused.

Claudia sensed his gaze upon her and wished he would not tease so. "Will you join us for tea, Vicar Woodley?"

"With pleasure, dear lady." He drew up a chair with the ease of one who does that sort of thing often.

Claudia happened to glance at her friend and noted Olivia's cheeks were flushed and her manner slightly flustered. Olivia nurtured a *tendre* for the vicar, poor dear. Olivia poured from the fresh pot of tea brought in by the vigilant Mrs. Tibbins, offering a cup to the vicar with hesitant admiration.

"How do you like living in the country, vicar?" The smooth tones coming from Lord Hawke would have lured anyone less sharp into possibly making an indiscreet comment. Not Vicar Woodley.

"This is a charming community with much to admire. Lady Fairfax is the leading light roundabout. If you want something done, one only needs to apply to her gracious person and she sees that it is done." His smile was obsequious.

"Except for ponies, perhaps," the viscount murmured.

Fortunately Olivia chose that moment to inquire

about the coming social at the church to raise funds for repair of the steeple. Edward got down from his steed to sneak a pastry.

"The dear ladies of this church intend to make it a fête champêtre. Mrs. Alcock attended that sort of elaborate breakfast while in London and thought the idea commendable."

"Pity you do not have a lake to use. A water party would have been charming," Lord Hawke inserted. "Although perhaps a river serves more admirably for those affairs," he concluded with a reflective tone.

Claudia longed to poke him with her elbow. He was sitting close enough to her to make it a simple matter. "I think the desire to raise funds for the steeple repair a worthy one. I trust you will attend the fête, my lord?" She turned to bestow a smile on him that was quite as false as that silly reflective attitude he assumed.

It was not the smartest thing she had done in a while. He seemed to move closer to her, although she would have sworn he remained still. Those intensely blue eyes bore into her with faint amusement. "I shall be pleased to escort you—all."

The vicar looked disappointed.

"Will they have donkey rides?" Edward inquired in his high fluting voice.

"That is a good thought. I will mention it to one of the committee." The vicar set his cup down, then rose. Taking Edward by the hand he began to lead him to the door. "I suppose we had best go over your Latin, my boy."

"I could show you how well I ride on my new rocking horse," Edward said in an effort to stave off the inevitable.

"It is a fine one, to be sure," the vicar agreed.

"Lord Hawke brought it for Edward. He is always so kind and generous," Olivia said after quickly rising to her feet as well.

She walked to the door with them. "I will help with

Edward's papers. You know how boys can be—not always tidy."

The three left the room together, their voices fading as they went up the stairs to the boy's rooms.

The snapping of a log in the fireplace broke the utter silence that descended at their departure.

"I find it hard to believe that your dragon would leave you to my not-so-tender mercies, Claudia." Lord Hawke shifted so he might better converse with her. His movement brought his knee in contact with hers.

She jumped like a shy virgin. Ignoring the smirk that briefly crossed his lips, Claudia shifted away from him. Then she rose to her feet turning back to gaze at him with what she hoped was a demure smile. His use of her given name did not escape her notice. "Sir, you are too familiar. What would the good vicar think should he hear you?"

"He would assume that our many years of association, as well as my being Edward's guardian—"

"Coguardian," Claudia inserted swiftly.

"Coguardian," he amended, "would permit friendly terms between us." His eyes gleamed with wicked mischief.

"Be that as it may, I will not have you bandying my given name about." She gave him an obstinate look.

"I have given you leave to use mine," he pointed out, sounding like a boy bargaining for a sweet.

"I refuse to use it. It isn't seemly, and you know it." Claudia felt like stamping her foot in annoyance. Dear heaven but this man could drive her mad.

He rose, paused at her side as though debating a point, then bowed slightly. "I shall bid you good day, my dear Lady Fairfax. Edward shall have his pony within a week. But I shall return. To see my ward, of course."

Claudia hoped that was all he had in mind.

Chapter Two

*C*laudia listened to the snap of the front door closing as Lord Hawke left the house. She let out a breath she wasn't aware she had been holding. Gracious, her husband had never affected her so! She was an utter ninnyhammer to permit "that man" to rattle her nerves.

Olivia was still upstairs with the vicar and Edward. She would not return until the vicar left or he possibly dismissed her. Since Claudia suspected he enjoyed the admiration of a lady—any lady—she doubted that would happen. If only the vicar didn't break Olivia's heart.

Catching up her elderly shawl, she wandered to the back of the house, leaving by a side door for the freedom of the garden. The sullen gray clouds were now allowing a glimpse of clear blue sky and shafts of sunlight. The day had suddenly become most promising.

She walked along the gravel path, her feet crunching loudly in the silence that had followed the storm. Water dripped from the leaves, a near-silent echo of the rain.

The roses had faded months ago, the leaves now a dull green, some mildewed. Great globes of blue hydrangeas sent showers at every touch as she passed them. From the dancing fuchsia blooms tiny diamond drops dangled, sparkling as a shard of afternoon sun blessed them. In the grove of trees beyond the kitchen garden a flock of sparrows settled, resting on their flight south. She could hear goldfinches in the not too distant field, noisily feasting on the abundant seed of the thistles.

It soothed her nerves.

She walked on along the paths she had grown to know so well these past months. The garden had been a balm in her distress, a delight to her eyes.

At last she decided she had recovered sufficiently to have a word with Jem Groom regarding the pony. She knew full well that Lord Hawke would stand by his promise to buy a pony for Edward. His lordship did not make idle threats.

She swung open the tall garden gate to the busy environment of the stable yard. The sight of his curricle revealed that Lord Hawke had not left. She paused, irresolute. She did not want to confront him again. Before she could retreat to her garden, he appeared.

The man who stopped a moment to add a few words to someone in the interior—Jem, most likely—was quite unlike her late husband. The viscount had the broad shoulders, trim hips, lean, yet powerful form aspired to by younger men. That stylish hat he had set atop his dark hair completed his smart appearance. Her late husband—stout, out of fashion in his attire, sparse of hair—had been the direct opposite of the dashing Lord Hawke.

Lord Hawke frightened her. He also sent tremors shooting through her body in a most alarming manner. She sensed she should not be alone with him and not just for propriety's sake. She wasn't a coward usually. Only when it came to intimidating, infuriating men did she quail. Namely, Lord Hawke.

Before she could achieve her retreat he caught sight of her and she found herself trapped. On the one hand she feared his assault on her nerves, on the other, she did not want him to realize how badly he affected her. She would not give him the satisfaction of sending her into a panicked withdrawal.

"We meet again," he said in that rich, deep voice she reluctantly admired. "Was there something you wished to add to our previous conversation?"

"I thought you had left, sir. I wanted a word with Jem Groom." She hated the defensive note in her voice. It would not do to allow him to think she feared him.

"He and I agree on the pony. You failed to tell me that he urged you to buy a pony for Edward some time ago." He walked closer to where she stood by the garden gate until he loomed over her, causing her to wish she had managed her escape. Really, the man was too devastating.

"You fail to understand the root of my fears," she retorted with ill-advised heat. More quietly she continued. "I have my reasons. But I confess you have the right of it. Edward must learn to ride. Jem will be an excellent teacher." She hoped this admission would satisfy his lordship and send him on his way.

"I imagine so. And you, madam? Will you ride with your stepson?" He tilted his head to study her.

"You must have learned from Jem that I do not ride."

"Rubbish! I will make a point of joining you and Edward in frequent rides. Have your maid brush off your riding habit," he commanded.

"No man gives me orders, my lord. In particular, *you* have no authority to do so. *If* I decide to ride again, and with *Edward,* it will be because *he* wishes it, or *I* choose to ride the docile mare that has been mine in the past."

He drew in a deep breath. "By heavens, you need someone to tame you, madam."

"Truly? Well, it won't be you!" With that pungent retort, she backed up to the garden gate, fumbled until she found the latch, then opened it. Her intent to escape her tormentor was foiled when he crossed the few steps now separating them and entered the silent world of her garden with her.

He stood at her side, examining her with narrow eyes, deep in thought. "What makes you fight me?"

"Fight, sir? I fight with no one. I am a peace-loving woman. Surely you make more from our words than is warranted?" She flashed him an intrepid look.

He firmed his lips, then took a step that brought him up against her. Claudia suddenly realized how slender and frail she was next to him. It was like a green reed standing up to an oak!

"So you love peace? What else do you love, widow?" His voice had dropped to a low growl, like that of a predatory cat.

"My privacy." She stepped back from him. He followed. "My lord, you intrude on both my peace and privacy."

He smiled a lopsided, lethal grin that warned and yet challenged her.

"May I suggest you leave now?" she dared to advise.

"I will . . . eventually." He made no move to depart.

She licked her suddenly dry lips, wondering how to deal with this man. Her pulse galloped madly. He was a menace, a peril to her hard-won tranquillity.

Without warning, he dipped his head and kissed her. Her traitorous lips responded. They had been neglected for years and welcomed the firm lips that touched hers. She ought to back away, to join the fluttering butterflies on the far side of the garden. She would be in like company, for her innards gamboled like a lamb let out to pasture.

It didn't last long, that stolen kiss. He drew away from her, examining her from those intensely blue eyes with disconcerting thoroughness. "You kiss like a spinster. Did your husband not teach you how a married woman kisses?"

Angry at his taunting, she unwisely snapped, "My husband taught me nothing."

The smile that caught in his eyes cautioned her to close her mouth. She said rash things when infuriated, and this particular man could drive her mad with little effort.

"I agree."

Defensive, she glared at her adversary. "I should not think a wife required tutorage in kissing, or anything else, for that matter. I was an obedient wife, doing all required of me."

His hand reached out to gently trail a line down her cheek before he cupped her chin. "Someday you will know."

When he dropped his hand to his side her skin felt bereft. Silly, stupid woman that she was, she found she longed for a man's gentle touch, kisses, the other things she had missed during her married life.

She looked behind him through to the stable yard where Lord Hawke's carriage stood. "Your curricle awaits you."

After a look that seemed to strip her soul bare, he left her, crossing the yard in long strides as though he couldn't get away from her fast enough.

Claudia glanced at the butterflies. Red admirals, if she was not mistaken. They seemed unaffected by anything. A gentle breeze wafted through the garden, tossing the hydrangea blooms and causing the fuchsia to dance as though to some wild Scottish reel. Entering the kitchen garden she found an early pippin apple and picked it.

The crunch of her teeth in the firm flesh of the apple was a satisfying sound. Her bite was savage, as though she punished the viscount rather than a mere apple. It had a not unpleasant tang. Unlike the viscount, she thought.

Olivia was still with the vicar and Edward when Claudia reentered the house. She paused in consideration. It would be wise to invite a friend to visit. She needed a buffer from her neighbor, for she held no illusion he would not return now that he had his way regarding the pony. There was still Eton to settle. And lessons, perhaps? a wayward voice inserted in the back of her mind.

After thinking a moment she went to her little desk. Setting her drawings to one side, she found a piece of writing paper and a good pen. She wrote her letter, and when done, she took it to Jem Groom to mail for her in the village.

Adela, Lady Dunston, was an especially dear friend, one who had offered comfort following the tragic death of Lord Fairfax. She had understood what Claudia endured for she was also a widow, having married a man who was mad for hunting to the cost of his life. Claudia had no doubt that she would come at once given the message sent to her. A slow grin crossed Claudia's face as she crunched the rest of her pippin. It was a delight to thwart the desires of Lord Hawke, for desires she knew he had. She had seen them in those deep blue eyes of his. Of her own desires she stubbornly chose to remain ignorant.

Noel drove along the lane to his property deeply in thought. The widow proved far more enticing than he remembered, and he had nursed fond memories of her, her golden curls and fine blue eyes—as her stepson called them—all the months he had been in London. She'd spoiled him for others.

That she could be so untouched, so virginal in her responses was beyond belief. Yet he knew about the late Lord Fairfax's mistress and their several children living in the next village. They were far enough removed to avoid the worst of gossip, yet close enough for his convenience. And near enough so word of their existence reached Lady Fairfax, he was certain. She had taken his lordship's death with superb calm. Yet he knew she simmered with emotions. He had scarcely begun to explore them and he longed to delve deeper.

Upon reaching his home, he handed the reins to his groom, then strode inside, intent upon what needed doing next. Eton. The boy had to have the benefit of other boys his age. True, he was a bit on the frail side, but Eton and the life there would toughen him up. As well, he would make friends that would last him all his life.

Once in his library, Noel flung himself into the large leather chair behind his desk to mull over the matter. Finally his brow cleared and he pulled a piece of hot-pressed paper from a drawer to compose a carefully thought out letter to a good friend. Maximilian, Viscount Elliot, had been with Noel at Eton. No one was a better friend. He would help set the widow straight on the matter. Two against one! Those were odds Noel could like.

His feelings for the widow Fairfax were complex. He first admired her cool beauty, though his admiration had slowly turned to more as time passed. While it was a pity the old roué had passed on to his reward when his carriage turned over, Noel could not sincerely mourn his death. Any man who could treat a lovely young woman as he had, turning instead to the blowsy charm of the widow Norton, was beyond Noel. Mrs. Norton had borne two girls following Fairfax's marriage to Claudia, making four children in all. Unforgivable.

That he had not bothered to tutor his young wife in the delights of the marriage bed, or of marriage itself, was a crime. Noel couldn't know this for certain, of course. But his stolen kiss had told him much. There had been a kind of yearning in her response. He had not missed her leaning into him, her breathless gaze when he withdrew. She hadn't slapped him. The neglect to retaliate was curious. She ought to have been furious with him. She had been in a state of shock . . . or something.

He concluded his letter and sealed it with a blob of red wax before impressing his signet. How Max would grin at that.

The remainder of his afternoon was spent on the estate work that piled up while he was in London. His steward was a good man, sent faithful reports and letters with queries. However, it was at times necessary to personally attend to matters. He did so now. But he intended to see the widow as soon as possible.

When finished he went to his bedroom and from a drawer pulled a gorgeous length of fabric. It was an extremely fine Paisley shawl. The rich colors would enhance the widow's delicate beauty. It would replace that shabby thing she had worn earlier. She deserved better, and he owed her an apology. He intended to see that she got all she deserved.

Vicar Woodley left not long after Claudia had endured the scene with Viscount Hawke. The vicar had paused in the front hall, lingering perhaps in the hope of being invited to dine at Fairfax Hall. She wished to talk with Olivia alone, without the danger of other ears hearing what she had to say. At last he left.

Olivia was decidedly put out. "Claudia, I believe the vicar wished to remain with us." Olivia seated herself primly on the far end of the sofa, sounding quite annoyed.

"No doubt he did. I wished to have a private time with you, my dear. He can dine here another day."

"Oh . . . how good. I am certain he does not fare so well at any other house." She gave Claudia an uncertain look.

Mrs. Tibbins entered the room. "Dinner is served, madam."

"What a strange mood you are in, dear Claudia."

Olivia sent a perplexed look at her friend as they entered the dining room.

"I have done something with which I hope you approve."

"A pony for Edward? I suspected that man would persuade you. Heavens, fancy having to deal with him until Edward is of age! I do not envy you in the least."

"Indeed, I capitulated on the pony. It is time and more that he learn to ride. It was only . . ."

"I understand." Olivia reached out to pat Claudia's hand in sympathy as they entered the dining room.

"Actually, what I wish to tell you is that I wrote a letter to invite Lady Dunston to come for a visit. Adela will be a help. Not that you aren't, dear girl. But with your assisting the vicar during Edward's lessons, well, I am left at the mercy of that man should he appear like he did today."

"His lordship left around the time we went to Edward's rooms, did he not?"

"He went to see Jem Groom regarding the pony. Jem let it slip that he had advised me to purchase a pony for Edward some time ago. Jem also informed his lordship that I have not been riding. Accordingly, Lord Hawke told me that he would be over to ride with Edward and me . . . daily, if the man is to be believed!"

"Merciful heaven," Olivia said on a gasp.

"He does like to hand out orders."

"I cannot believe you permitted him to order you about like that." Olivia finished off her mushroom soup, then daintily blotted her lips.

"Nor can I," Claudia replied with a heartfelt sigh.

"I saw you had that old shawl out again. You really ought to consign it to the ragbag. I know you have a nicer one. What would your neighbor say were he to see you wearing that old thing wrapped about you?"

Claudia said nothing about that neighbor's reaction

to her in the garden. She didn't want Olivia to have an attack of the vapors during the middle of dinner.

The soup was removed with a neat dish of salmon. This was followed by an assortment of roast duck, a ragout of pork, and assorted vegetables—Olivia being convinced it was a wise thing to do for their health.

They were both toying with their delicate sponge cake when Olivia brought up the matter of Lady Dunston. "She is very smart. I daresay she will find us rather dull after her time in London." Was there a hint of jealousy there?

"Adela is not the sort of woman who must have constant entertainment. Have you forgotten how kind she was to me after Lord Fairfax's death? As a widow she understood precisely what problems I faced. She gave me excellent advice, which I followed."

Olivia relented, for she was too kindhearted to think ill of anyone for long. "True," she admitted. "However, the vicar seems to come more often than he did early on."

"Indeed." The poor dear sounded too hopeful, yet Claudia was reluctant to dash her longings. "I wish Lord Hawke would go far, far away. Then I'd not have to be vexed when he shows up, as he is bound to do. And probably more often than I would wish. As you once said, he is a disturbing man."

"We would often be sorry if our wishes were gratified," Olivia primly intoned. "Aesop offers many wise sayings."

"Oh, is Edward into Aesop at this point? In Greek or Latin? Latin, I suppose." Claudia looked up from the last crumb of her sponge, wondering if she should have a second piece. She decided to indulge herself and took another helping, pouring raspberry sauce over the slice with anticipation.

Olivia blushed. "Indeed. I am learning along with the boy and was able to translate the line without fault."

"I am sure Vicar Woodley was pleased."

"He is the best of teachers."

"Olivia . . ." Claudia stopped. How could she caution her friend regarding a love that was not returned? Olivia looked at her with a faint frown, a question in her eyes. "Take care, my dearest friend. I would not have you hurt."

"Oh, I know a man like the vicar would never look twice at me. He is so handsome and could have almost any lady he pleased. I do believe he intends to marry. He said something about the vicarage needing the attention of a woman." Olivia's color deepened. "I confess I longed to tell him I would do quite well in the role."

Of course she had the right of it all, but Claudia refused to agree with her. After all, miracles happened. "You never know, dear. God works in mysterious ways." Then she wondered if someone ought to let the vicar know about Olivia's legacy.

They left the dining room to sit by the comforting blaze of the sitting room fire. Both women had much to think about and were ready for bed early.

Claudia rose first, going up to find Edward still awake.

"Lord Hawke said he is going to find me a pony, Mama. Do you very much dislike my having a pony? I will be very careful and not fall off." He bestowed an earnest look on her.

"You will be a topping rider, and if you fall, it will undoubtedly be the pony's fault. Have you thought of a name?" She knew guilt for preventing his riding. The sooner he had his pony, the better it would be.

"Well, the vicar said it was all humbug, so perhaps I will call the pony Humbug?"

"That is certainly an original name." She shared a grin with her stepson, a moment of pleasant harmony.

Edward said his prayers. Claudia kissed his cheek, then went to her own bed. Her sleep was slow in coming.

*   *   *

A lovely autumn morning greeted her upon rising. The sunshine brought mellow tones to the grass, highlighting the late daisies. Wood smoke drifted through the tranquil air.

She strolled through the grounds before the house, inspecting the various plants. Suddenly she heard the approach of a carriage. Just why she suspected it might be Hawke, she couldn't say. Somehow she knew it was.

He sped up the gravel drive until he drew abreast of her. "Madam, I trust I find you in good health today?"

She curtsied politely and agreed she was fine.

After turning the reins over to his groom, he joined her on the lawn. He carried a modest package. "I have come to make amends for my behavior yesterday. Here." He opened the paper to reveal a magnificent shawl.

Claudia gasped. "I do not think your manners warrant *this*. But I thank you for the thought. I cannot accept it."

"Nonsense. You'd not wish to anger me, now would you?" He draped the shawl about her. "Beautiful."

She wondered if he meant the shawl or her humble self. It was extremely difficult to reject such an offering. And, she reasoned, he *had* offended her yesterday. This was a handsome apology. Too much so! "It is too much, my lord."

"I like how it looks on you—precisely as I envisioned. You will accept it and wear it in good health."

"You are ordering again." She flashed him a warning look.

He smiled. "You are being stubborn. Accept my gift in the spirit in which it is given."

It was a beautiful shawl. "Thank you, Lord Hawke."

A robin trilled a note. The sparrows took wing, their flight a great rush of sound. In the field the chattering goldfinch continued to feast on thistle seed.

Chapter Three

A sudden chill had descended on Claudia even as she felt the warmth of the shawl around her shoulders. It was an inward chill, rather unpleasant. Why did Lord Hawke seek to gain her favor with the gift of a shawl? Was it something he wanted from her? Other than sending Edward to Eton this autumn? And why was he so insistent that Edward depart so soon? He could be gone in a month or two. She would miss the lad frightfully.

She glanced at the man so casually strolling along at her side. What went on in his scheming mind? It was a pity he was so devilishly attractive. It would be easier to reprimand a person for whom one felt repulsion. Lord Hawke was too handsome for her peace of mind. Possibly his, as well, come to think about it. He would have the girls making their come-outs in London pursuing him—intent upon snaring him like some prime rabbit.

"The shawl is too fine and far too expensive a gift for such a *minor* infraction. I would welcome a simple apology. That is sufficient." She stressed the word minor. Let him think she thought nothing of his kiss.

"I apologize. It was not well done of me to succumb to your charms like that. You are a very enticing woman, you know." His expression was bland, but she got a glimpse of his eyes and suspected he was inwardly amused. "But I insist you keep the shawl. I have no need for such. Besides, you are the step-mother of my ward. We have a different relationship than mere friends."

Claudia shot him a suspicious glance. "We do?"

"I should say we have, ah, more liberty." He paused to look down at her, that lopsided smile that had been so devastating yesterday assaulting her nerves again.

"You have tested that to the limit, I should think." Claudia tried to shut her mind to the tantalizing kiss he had bestowed on her the day before. A small part of her wanted to show this man that she did *not* kiss like a spinster. The rest of her said to leave well enough alone. "Actually, I believe it is guardians," she concluded in a cool, distant manner.

"He is your stepson and my godson, so we are in lieu of parents, are we not?" He spoke with simple logic, sounding not a little like Edward at his most persuasive.

She nodded reluctantly. "I suppose you might con-strue it in that light." She took a calming breath. "What has brought you to the country?" She knew well enough he possessed several estates, of which this was a minor one, or so she'd been told.

She also knew better than to think he had come here on her account. What would any man of his stamp find appealing about a woman whose husband had found her so wanting? Yet Olivia's words lingered in Claudia's mind. Her year of mourning was up. She was free to remarry should she want to do something so foolish. She had received a tidy portion of land as part of her jointure. Since it marched with Lord Hawke's property, it might well be a target for his interest. Not her, never her.

"There are matters that called for my attention." He said no more, allowing Claudia's mind to grapple with possibilities.

She nibbled her lower lip, wondering how much to

say. "I do hope that they are not too onerous and that you will be able to go hunting . . . if that is what you enjoy in the autumn."

"I like to hunt as well as the next man." He touched her elbow, guiding her around the end of the side garden.

Claudia paused by a clump of foxglove, bending to strip seed from a stalk. The action enabled her to be free of his touch. As sure as she breathed there was a hint, an innuendo in those words. She didn't dare ask him *what* he liked to hunt. Her voice was likely to be a tremor, for his touch had far too much affect on her. And she was twenty-seven? She was reacting like a foolish child of seventeen.

"Lord Hawke, I didn't know you had come!" Edward caroled as he galloped around from the back of the house. He ended his precipitate rush by hurling himself against Claudia.

Bless her stepson's heart. Claudia welcomed his intrusion, even if he nearly bowled her over.

"Good morning, my lad." His lordship reached to tousle the boy's hair and draw him away from his stepmother. "Have you been practicing on your rocking horse? I have it on good authority that a handsome pony is available and should be here this week."

"Humbug!" Edward cried with glee.

Lord Hawke gave Claudia a puzzled look. "Humbug?" he echoed.

She had to laugh. "The vicar said a pony was all humbug, and nothing will do but for Edward to name his pony Humbug."

"I suppose there are worse names for a pony. But why not Valiant or some brave name?" Lord Hawke looked perplexed.

"He has his heart set on Humbug, and Humbug it will be." Claudia laughed again at the expression on his lordship's face. "And I agree, it could be worse."

"What would be worse, Mama?" Edward demanded

to know, turning his attention from a strange insect to the adults.

"Never mind. Would you like to show Lord Hawke your new swing?" She thought it best to divert both males—Edward from pursuing that thought and Hawke from grasping her elbow again, an elbow that had by now become a sensory target for far too many nerves.

Lord Hawke gave her a knowing look that told her he knew precisely why she was sending them off. To confound him, she continued to walk at his side, only a trifle more distant. When they reached the tall oak from which Jem had suspended stout ropes, she stopped.

"Push me, please," Edward demanded politely. "Mama tries but I bet you can push me higher."

"Schemer," his lordship muttered half under his breath.

"Should I say that it takes one to know one, sir?" Claudia replied with composure.

Hawke amiably pushed his godson on the swing, inwardly castigating himself for yesterday's kiss. He had done stupid things in his day, but that was beyond stupid. The very desirable widow Fairfax was more skittish than ever. He suspected she had never been truly comfortable in his company. He was so vastly different from her late husband.

As far as Hawke could tell, the late Lord Fairfax had valued his wife merely as an unpaid governess and substitute mother for his young son. It was a pity that the lovely Claudia had not borne him a child. Which gave rise to speculation as to whether or not she could. Baron Fairfax had fathered four children on the widow Norton in addition to the one his first wife had given him. Claudia had none. Was it for lack of effort on the late baron's part? Hawke hoped so.

He cast another glance at the beautiful widow. She wore an adorably confused expression on her face. He suddenly realized all was not lost in her regard. He might gain a position of trust if he concentrated on Edward and included Claudia on the planning. He would persuade her to participate in various events, like teaching Edward to ride. It was evident that unless he pretended little interest in her, it would be difficult for him to spend any time with her at all.

He gave Edward a push that sent the lad sailing high in the air. Turning to Claudia, he said in a quiet, confiding manner, "We had best arrive at a plan for teaching Edward to ride before that pony comes at the end of the week. Do you have any ideas?"

"No, not really." She took another step away from him.

Not only did she seem suspicious, she had a mutinous tilt to her lips—those luscious lips he had tasted so briefly the day before. When would he have another chance? He had muffed things badly. It merely proved how a man's desire could overrule his brain when it came to a beautiful woman. He had admired her for far too long to be discouraged now. He had the advantage of a legitimate entrée to her company— her stepson. He would concentrate on that. Once he earned the widow's trust, he had things in mind for her. He smiled at the mental image.

Claudia retreated from his lordship, intent upon keeping her distance. He could talk about planning for Edward. However, if he sent the boy off to Eton there would be no need for that. It gave her pause. Perhaps she ought to compromise? As soon as the vicar indicated that Edward was ready to attend the school, she could send her precious boy off into a cold world to fend for himself, managing bullies, illtempered teachers . . . No, how could she? It would be too cruel to a young, sensitive child.

She retreated another step, tripping over a root that stuck up just far enough to accomplish the deed. She fell, twisting her ankle, causing dreadful pain. At her cry of alarm, the viscount spun away from the swing to rush to her aid.

"Are you all right?"

Claudia thought he sounded genuinely concerned. Was he? Or was he merely trying to restore himself in her good graces? Not that he was ever there, mind you.

"It is nothing, I assure you," she hastened to inform the intimidating gentleman who assisted her to her feet.

"I do not think so. Can you take a step on your own?"

Claudia tried to ignore the faint throb in her ankle and bravely stepped forward. "Ouch!" She hadn't been able to prevent the exclamation from escaping. She must have twisted her ankle badly to cause such discomfort.

He didn't give her a chance to object, but quickly gathered her into his arms. "Come, Edward, I shall need your help."

The notion that anyone as splendid as Lord Hawke might need his assistance entranced the boy so that he ran along at his hero's side as they made for the house.

Claudia inhaled the tangy scent of his shaving soap and the costmary fragrance that clung to his shirt. Her husband had disdained such fripperies as scents of any kind. However, these were nice, and not the least feminine. At least not on someone as masculine as Lord Hawke. She could not help but lean against that well-muscled chest. Had her husband found her in like circumstance he couldn't have picked her up to carry her even a foot. He had enjoyed his food too much. She discovered being held close in Hawke's arms a pleasurable experience. She admitted she liked the man—perhaps even more. There had been moments in the past when she'd shared a look with him that had stirred something deep within her. She had buried it until now.

"Mama, I will tell Cousin Olivia that you are hurt."

Before she could reply, Edward dashed off to the house, calling for "Cousin Olivia" at the top of his lungs.

"Oh, dear," Claudia said with a sigh. "She will be so upset. She is very sensitive."

"And you are not? I congratulate myself that you are losing your fear of me." Lord Hawke cradled her carefully against him.

There was more than a hint of laughter in his voice and she knew an urge to dig her elbow into that solid, muscular chest of his. She had never seen her husband without his nightshirt or unless he was fully clothed. But she could feel, and what she felt now was firm rather than rolls of fat. There was undoubtedly not an ounce of excess fat on Lord Hawke.

She darted a glance up at his face. He looked to be enjoying himself! "I wish you might put me down. I fear I am too much a burden for you. Could I not walk with your help at one side? After all, it is only the one ankle that is injured."

"You? A burden? Never, fair lady. You are a delightful armful, if I am permitted to say such a thing without offense." He held her even closer. She felt cherished.

Claudia stared at the front door as they neared it. Before she could reply, Olivia burst forth, her hands in a flutter.

"Oh, my dear Claudia, what has happened? Edward said you fell. How fortunate that Lord Hawke was able to bring you to the house. Should I summon the apothecary? Mr. Beemish might be available." She wrung her hands while hovering in anxiety.

"Mr. Beemish is not needed. I sustained nothing

more than a slight sprain. A cool cloth will do nicely. Just place me on the sofa in the little sitting room. That will be most convenient."

"And elevate your foot, ma'am." The viscount spoke with a sober mien, his tone and features revealing nothing. His eyes, however, were laughing at her and she longed to do something to punish the man. What for, she couldn't say.

"As you say, Lord Hawke." She gave him a demure nod. The aching bothered her a bit more now. How odd it was that pain in an ankle could affect how one felt all over.

He placed her on the sofa with the greatest of care, quite as though she was a priceless bit of art.

"I do wonder how you will be able to go to your bedroom. That swelling is not going to go down quickly. I shall stay for a time, then carry you upstairs when you wish to retire."

Claudia compressed her lips. How that man could vex her! "Surely Jem Groom might . . ." If Hawke stayed it would mean his company for dinner and unless she went to bed very early, also his company for a time in the evening. Drat!

"Claudia!" Olivia cried in a small voice. "*Not* Jem Groom! It truly would not be proper."

"We must be proper, my lady," Lord Hawke intoned gravely.

Olivia shot him an approving look. "You have the right of it, my lord. You know how gossip can damage a lady's reputation. A young and beautiful widow must be especially careful. It would be seemly for you to assist, as you are Edward's guardian."

"And that puts me above reproach?" He had the innocent air of a choirboy.

Claudia hardly knew where to look. Those intensely blue eyes were alive with humor. He laughed inwardly, and the worst of it was that she didn't blame him one bit. One minute Olivia had been castigating him to high heaven. All of a sudden he had acquired near sainthood. It was too much. Claudia chuckled.

"Dear, are you all right?" Olivia placed her hand on Claudia's forehead as though it was her head not her foot that had been injured.

"Perhaps a cup of tea would be welcome? My mother always says it works wonders for the nerves." Hawke stepped away from the sofa to survey Claudia from a short distance. Not far enough for her peace of mind, however.

"The very thing," Olivia cried. Before Claudia could tell her to summon Mrs. Tibbins, the dear girl whirled about and disappeared in a trice leaving Claudia and Lord Hawke together with Edward hanging over the end of the sofa.

"You said that on purpose," Claudia accused, but very quietly so that her words wouldn't carry far.

"I did," he agreed. "She needed to be doing something useful."

Claudia considered his words. They were true enough. She had seen more and more often that Olivia was not content unless she was performing some task for Claudia. At times, it was difficult to find an appropriate chore. However, she was surprised that Lord Hawke had noticed such a thing so quickly.

"Your mother's wisdom again?"

"If you like." He took the chair opposite to where she reclined. He studied her with seeming care. She was disconcerted when he rose. A few steps and he stood by her swollen ankle. He gently removed her Roman slipper, unlacing it with tender regard for her pain. Then he found two pillows and deftly tucked them under her foot, elevating it just as it ought to be.

"Thank you," she said, although wincing with the discomfort of having anyone handle her aching extremity.

"I am but your humble servant, my lady."

"Ha! I doubt you have had a humble day in all your life," Claudia snapped before she realized how ungracious her words were. "Forgive me. It must be the pain in my foot that is causing me to forget my manners."

"Does it hurt much, Mama?" Edward asked, looking worried.

"A little more than I like, dear." She would not deceive the lad. Perhaps it would teach him a lesson in taking care.

Lord Hawke settled back in the chair once again, covering his mouth behind which lurked whatever expression he wore.

Mrs. Tibbins entered to leave a tea tray for them. Olivia followed with a bowl of cool water. She wrung out a small cloth and gently placed it over the injured limb.

The viscount rose to quietly speak with the housekeeper. When he finished, she nodded, then disappeared at once on some errand for him. What, Claudia couldn't imagine.

"Mrs. Tibbins is of the opinion that an early dinner and an equally early bed for you would be in your best interest."

"I suppose you added that you will remain until it is time for me to go up to my room?" Claudia inquired, her manner as demure as a prim miss.

"Of course, he must stay, dearest Claudia. I will consult with Mrs. Tibbins regarding the meal. Never fear, all will be as you would wish." Olivia popped up from where she had perched on a side chair. After brief inspection of the injured ankle she was off in the direction of the kitchen.

Claudia shook her head, making a wry face at this turn of events. "As you said, Olivia does like to keep busy."

"I daresay you do as well. Will you find it difficult to be off your feet for a time? I doubt you will find it comfortable to walk for a few days." He thoughtfully poured her tea, adding the bit of sugar she liked. She gave him high marks for being observant. He brought it to her, assisting her to sip the hot beverage. Only by concentrating on the tea and ignoring him was she able to reply.

Thinking of the sketching she wished to finish, she shook her head. "Not as long as I have a pad and pencil to hand. I promised Edward to draw him a dragon."

"But you draw fairies." His gaze was watchful and curious.

She took a deep breath, looking up at the ceiling before attempting a reply. "I like to draw fanciful creatures. Fairies are charming sprites, dainty and delicately lovely. True, the dragon is none of those, but you must admit it is whimsical."

"I had not thought you one who would create imaginary beings. In the past you always seemed so practical."

"I was unaware you noticed how I seemed. You usually came to see my husband . . . and Edward. We rarely spoke." She bestowed a curious look on him. Had he truly paid her the slightest regard?

There seemed to be no answer to this. He placed her teacup on the nearest table, then took the cloth from her ankle. He plunged it into the cool water, wrung it out, and then replaced it on her aching limb. "If I know anything of Mrs. Tibbins's skills, I would wager she put some herbs in that water to aid in soothing your ankle." He smoothed the cloth out, perhaps lingering a trifle longer than strictly necessary.

"Edward, perhaps Mrs. Tibbins would have a few sweet biscuits for us?" Lord Hawke smiled at the lad. "Would you be so kind as to ask?"

The thought of ginger biscuits brought a beatific smile to the small, slender boy. "At once, sir." He dashed from the room on his errand with the enthusiasm of a knight on his quest.

"I propose the pony be brought over this coming weekend. Do you think it possible that your ankle will be sufficiently recovered that you might join us on his first attempt? I believe he would like for you to watch him above all things. He takes great pleasure in your approval."

Claudia found herself in a quandary. She had made little of her injury. Indeed, a day or two of rest, perhaps some firm strapping, and she would be able to move around. Most assuredly she would not require his lordship's assistance again! Yet could she involve herself in this project?

"I know he would like me to watch him," she admitted at last. "Perhaps if I sat on a chair not far from where he would be?" She doubted Lord Hawke would approve of her scheme.

He didn't. He slowly shook his head. "If possible it would be better were you to be on that docile mare you mentioned before. Or do you fear being on a horse again?"

"I have never been a great one for riding. I think that unless you learn as a child it is most difficult to master. I had little opportunity to ride before I came to Fairfax Hall."

"A pity," he murmured as the sound of steps in the hallway reached them. They both looked to the doorway expecting to see Edward and perhaps a maid come with a plate of ginger biscuits.

To Claudia's, and possibly Lord Hawke's, surprise, Edward entered with the vicar at his side.

"Lady Fairfax! Young Edward tells me you have been injured. What a dreadful development for you." He approached the sofa where Claudia reclined and bowed, surreptitiously eyeing her ankle.

"True, I won't be up to taking long walks in the

garden to sketch my fairies for a time." What imp nudged her to mention the fairies around the good vicar she couldn't imagine.

He stiffened. A cool look of disdain settled on his face. "It would be better if you completely forgot about such silly notions," he snapped.

"But Mama likes to paint fairies," Edward protested. "She promised to paint me a dragon as well. I shall have a fine plate for my breakfast with a wicked dragon grinning up at me. It will make my food taste all the better." He ignored the vicar's sniff to assist the maid with the plate of ginger biscuits plus the coffee the vicar enjoyed. Edward offered the biscuits to all, then plumped himself on the floor to devour several.

"How shall you manage, dear Lady Fairfax?" the vicar begged, daintily sipping his beverage.

"Lord Hawke will carry me to my room following dinner."

The vicar's look of dismay was comical. "No! That is, it simply would not be seemly."

"Cousin Olivia assured me it would be far more proper than to set Jem Groom at the task," Claudia said in her most demure voice. What possessed her to tease the vicar she couldn't say.

"I assure you, good Vicar Woodley, I shall take the greatest care of Lady Fairfax," Lord Hawke declared.

The vicar looked chastened and angry. Thwarted, too.

Chapter Four

*C*laudia sank against the pillows now tucked behind her back. What in the world had possessed her to cling to her nemesis as she had? While he now charmed the daylights out of Olivia and annoyed the vicar beyond belief, Claudia had a chance to study him as she pretended to close her eyes for a time—supposedly against pain.

Truth to tell her ankle did hurt, but this was a heaven-sent opportunity to examine Lord Hawke to find out why he had this strange effect on her. She had never been one to lean on any gentleman. Her husband had left her to her own devices shortly after they were wed. If anything came up, she had dealt with it on her own, which had given her the strength she needed after he had died. With the help of the bailiff, she managed quite as well as before. She'd kept abreast of developments in agriculture, debating such things as crop rotation and draining bottomland heretofore unproductive. She doubted Lord Hawke could approximate her knowledge, she thought smugly.

Admittedly, Hawke was as handsome as could stare. The vicar might cut a dash among the local belles. Lord Hawke undoubtedly cut a swathe through Society's select parties with no effort at all. Not that Claudia had any experience with London Society. But letters from her dear friend Adela had kept her informed of her neighbor's eminence among the *ton*. Rumors abounded concerning his amours.

While Adela, Lady Dunston, was a widow like Claudia, thanks to her late husband's position she traveled in the highest of circles. She and her husband had visited often the first years of Claudia's marriage, during which the two women became fast friends. Adela kept her friend posted on all that went on during the Season while deploring that Claudia preferred to remain in the country. Claudia doubted very much that any tidbit of gossip regarding Lord Hawke had been omitted in the frequent epistles. Adela saw him often and reported all she knew.

So why did Claudia succumb to his charm at the merest happening, like her fall? What must he have thought of her when she leaned into his body as she had, nestling against him like a chick into the soft feathers of a hen? For protection? Not likely.

"Claudia?" Olivia said loudly. "Are you able to eat a bite? Mrs. Tibbins thought to serve a light supper in here, to save you attempting the rigors of the dining room. You will have a tray and we will eat at the small table over here." She gestured to a table much used for games.

While Claudia had been utterly absorbed in her reflections concerning Lord Hawke, someone had set the table for three. All she had to do was nibble enough to allay Olivia's worries and it would be safe to retreat to her room.

She chanced to glance at Hawke only to encounter his stare. Naturally she had noticed his restrained and elegant garb earlier. Now she observed his almost predatory expression. He reminded her of the barn cat when it stalked a bird.

According to Adela's letters, Lord Hawke could marry where he pleased, dally with whomever he wished. He was seen with one woman after another. He exuded an aura of power and sensuality of a kind to draw any woman he wanted to his side. Witness the silly effect he had on her!

Claudia had heard nothing of any problems on his estate. At her request, her bailiff kept her informed of all that went on over there. His tenants were satisfied. The crops had done very well this year after last year's disastrous rain. The house appeared to be in excellent condition from all reports. The staff looked after the property with zealous care.

So why was he here?

"Claudia?"

"I am sorry, Olivia. Woolgathering, I fear. What you suggest is quite practical. Once I have had a bite to eat I shall retire. I am sure that come morning my ankle will be in fine fettle." Claudia fervently hoped that Lord Hawke had forgotten about carrying her to her room. "Even now it feels much better."

The vicar inhaled sharply. "I am surprised you did not summon Beemish. The apothecary ought to look over the injury. You cannot be too careful, Lady Fairfax." He glared at Lord Hawke as he spoke.

Claudia wasn't given to giggles, but his haughty pose made her long to give vent to her sense of the ridiculous. "I believe I have been most prudent, Vicar Woodley." Except, she mentally added, when it came to Lord Hawke.

Mrs. Tibbins fortuitously entered with trays of hot food, ending all discussion about the injury to Claudia's ankle.

She ate more than she had expected. Particularly with Lord Hawke seated at the table so that whenever she raised her gaze, he was precisely in her line of vision. The delicacies on her plate disappeared to Mrs. Tibbins's obvious satisfaction.

When the dessert plates had been cleared and the women sipped tea while the men enjoyed a glass of port, Claudia waited to see what would happen next.

Olivia and the vicar became involved in a discussion

of the church bell that appeared to have developed a crack.

Lord Hawke, glass of port in hand, wandered over to gaze down at Claudia. "You look tired."

"What a charming thing to say, my lord. Is that part of your famous address when in London? I hear you sweep all other gentlemen aside with your style." She should know nothing of his time in London. She wouldn't, save for Adela's letters.

"Hardly, and you should know it. I gather Lady Dunston keeps you au courant with Society doings?" He loomed over her, intimidating, yet far too attractive for her equanimity.

"That she does." Claudia decided that the less she said, the better off she might be.

The vicar rose from the table with Olivia hovering at his side. "Lady Fairfax, you will have difficulty attaining your room. Might I be of service?" He flicked a contemptuous look at Lord Hawke, quite obviously wanting to best him.

Claudia nearly grinned at Olivia's dismayed expression.

Lord Hawke turned his attention to the overweening vicar. He raised a brow in a manner that would have intimidated a man of lesser conceit. "I will carry Lady Fairfax to her room when she is ready to retire. After all, as her stepson's coguardian, I hold a unique position in this household." His remark implied that the vicar not only did not have a place at Fairfax Hall, he was being far too audacious to suggest he might perform such a personal duty.

The vicar reddened slightly, then bowed stiffly, and said his farewell. Accompanied by Olivia, he left the room, and presumably the house.

"Does that maggot bother you often, Claudia?" Hawke swirled the remaining port in his glass while he surveyed her recumbent form. He looked far too much like the lord of the manor to suit her.

"Not often enough to please Olivia. And I have not given you leave to use my Christian name, sirrah." It was difficult to give him the set-down he so deserved when she was stretched out on the sofa and he stood over her with that disquieting poise of his quite in place. She tightened her grasp on her teacup.

"So you have no, er, interest in the good vicar?" He totally ignored her complaint about his familiarity.

"Nothing more than as the shepherd of our local flock."

"He is interested in you, not Miss Greene." Hawke took another swallow of the excellent port her late husband had stored away in the cellars.

"I fear as much. I do all I can to depress his interest, believe me." She halted in her admission. What made her confide in Hawke? She never spoke like this to anyone.

"Good. Perhaps we may be able to think of a means to discourage him even more." Hawke drained his glass, then perched beside her on the sofa. The touch of his hand on her forehead startled her. She hadn't expected him to do that, not that she didn't find his touch tantalizing.

"I have no fever, I assure you." She tried to pull back but with the pillows in place, there was no place for retreat. If he didn't move, she would most assuredly develop a fever.

"You are flushed. I feared some complication had set in." He leaned over her as though to study her face more intently.

Suspicions ran rampant through her mind and she wished Olivia would return immediately rather than linger at the door with the vicar.

"You wish to retire, I'm sure. I trust Mrs. Tibbins will put a poultice on that sprain." He turned to study the elevated foot, the dampened cloth covering her ankle adequately. He set the empty wineglass on the table with a firm thunk.

Claudia hastened to assure him that Mrs. Tibbins would look after her with the best of care.

"Fine. You are exhausted. Bed for you, my dear." With no further warning, he rose, gathered her in his arms, and walked from the room as though she was no more than a feather. He cleverly canted her so that her foot did not touch the stair rail, for which she was grateful. He seemed to think of everything. She tried to keep her distance from that tempting torso, but he didn't make it easy. She seemed to fall against him whether she wanted to or not. As much as she delighted in that firm, muscular body, that way lay danger.

"Which room is yours?" At the top of the stairs he paused. From one end of the hall Edward's childish voice could be heard. Turning the opposite direction, Hawke stared down at Claudia, drawing her closer. "I do not read minds, more's the pity."

"Third door on the left. I ought to have told you." The house was too silent. Where were Olivia and Mrs. Tibbins? Why hadn't they appeared to supervise her transport? He nudged the door open, then after a glance about the room, crossed to gently deposit her on her comfortable bed. Her sensible cambric nightgown had been draped across the bed. She knew she blushed at this exposure of her intimate apparel. She supposed his amours donned far more exquisite costumes, if they wore anything at all. The thought brought more fire to her cheeks.

"This is your room? Of course, it must be. I had rather thought you would occupy the master suite." He seemed not to notice her discomposure, gazing about him with seeming interest. Her little desk was a jumble, a pair of slippers lay tumbled by an armchair, and her favorite bonnet perched on top of the chest of drawers. It was a room obviously lived in.

Stung by his tone, she snapped, "This is the room

I have occupied since my marriage, Lord Hawke, not that it is of the slightest importance to you."

"You do not have the least notion of what is important to me." He bent over her injured foot, then, after pushing her skirt aside, began peeling her stocking off, revealing a shocking amount of her leg in the process.

"My lord!" she began before he silenced her with a look. He dropped the pink silk stocking on the bed and bent to examine the injury.

"Your ankle is somewhat discolored. It is swollen, but not as bad as I feared. I should think that in a few days you will be almost back to normal." He withdrew his intimidating presence from the bed and her powerless person.

Mrs. Tibbins swept into the room, carrying a tray holding a bowl and a length of bandaging. "Now, good sir," she said with a beaming smile, "best leave her to me. I will have her back on her feet in no time. You plan to attend the fête? My lady will likely need a strong arm on which to lean."

Claudia was about to chastise her good housekeeper for her hinting when his lordship strolled to the door. "I will attend, and be certain I will see to it that Lady Fairfax does not overdo that day." With those outrageous words, he left the room.

In moments Claudia heard his steps on the stairs, followed by the closing of the front door.

"You ought not have spoken to his lordship in that manner, Mrs. Tibbins. It is possible he had other plans for the fête."

The housekeeper smiled. "I doubt it. From what little I knows, gentlemen do not get into such a taking over a lady in whom they have no interest. He will be here."

Claudia subsided, speculating on precisely what form that interest might take.

*   *   *

Noel rode home in an odd mixture of feelings. On the one hand he felt frustrated. It appeared his courtship of the lovely widow would require an enormous amount of patience, something he possessed in limited quantity. However, on the other hand, it would seem that no other potential suitor was on the horizon. For that, he was extremely thankful.

Once at Hawke's Rest he summoned his valet to the study, a favorite room in the house.

"Philpott, how do matters stand here?"

"Very good, my lord." The portly valet tugged at his gray waistcoat and stood very straight.

"You have found someone to keep an eye on Fairfax Hall?"

"Indeed, my lord. It seems that a sister to one of our grooms works as maid there, while one of the Hall's grooms is walking out with our dairy maid. You should receive daily news."

Noel fiddled with the pen on his desk, thinking. "Mind you, I'd not wish anyone to be aware of what I want to know."

"I took the liberty of letting it be known that you promised his late lordship that you would keep an eye on the widow once her year of mourning was up." The valet raised his gaze to the ceiling. "It would seem proper that you should vet any gentleman who seeks too close an interest in the fair lady."

Noel tossed the pen from him, frowning in thought. "I hope that will do. Very good, Philpott. Lady Fairfax has injured her ankle. I want to know if anything is amiss there."

Knowing himself dismissed, the valet silently departed from the library leaving Noel in peace, such as it was. It didn't last long.

A knock on the door heralded his head groom. "Begging your pardon, my lord, but the pony has arrived. Prime little fellow, it is. Traveled slow and easy."

Noel tucked his plans to the back of his mind, following his groom out of the house and back to the stables. As the groom said, the pony proved to be first-rate. A sly grin settled on Noel's face. The next few days ought to be intriguing. He had an excellent reason to be at the Hall, and he would make use of it.

The following morning Claudia managed to hop down the hall to the stairs without anyone the wiser. She plopped down at the top, then continued on her way, one step at a time on her bottom. The house was quiet; no one would know.

The front door opened silently and prickles rose on the back of her neck. Glancing up, she saw her neighbor standing in the morning light, hands on his hips, a forbidding frown on his face. Within seconds he was up the stairs and had gathered her in his arms.

"Have you no sense at all, woman?" With seeming ease he carried her to the main floor and around to the sitting room where she spent so much time. He gently set her on the sofa.

"Do you make a habit of marching into houses not your own, my lord?" Claudia's voice and manner came straight from a January storm.

"Mrs. Tibbins told me to go on into the house. I brought Edward's pony over. She thought you would wish to know at once. She had the right of it, didn't she?"

There was a hint of uncertainty in his voice. Claudia gave him a cautious look. "I would naturally be pleased to see Edward's new pony. I fear it will have to wait, however."

"Mama, Mama! Mrs. Tibbins said there is a pony in the stables. May I please go see it? Please?"

Claudia smiled at Edward. No matter how she might feel about Hawke, she would not hinder his kindness to her stepson.

"We shall all go out." Lord Hawke took a step toward her.

Before Claudia could protest, she was summarily picked up and whisked from the house. "Really, my lord, is this proper?" He shifted her in his arms, requiring that she cling to his neck lest she slip.

"Concerned about propriety, are you? I suppose you would rather the good vicar assisted you?" He fixed that intensely blue gaze on her and she felt all her qualms slither away.

"You know that is not the case. It is just . . . ." Claudia gave up, quite defeated before she might begin to scold his lordship. How could she reveal the truth of the matter? That every time he picked her up and held her close in his arms, she wanted a great deal more? The memory of that brief and chastising kiss lingered in her mind like a piece of bad plum cake that had settled in her stomach and refused to go away.

Hawke set her down on a chair mysteriously brought forth from somewhere, perhaps the kitchen. Edward danced around, impatient to see his pony. When Jem Groom brought it forth she couldn't resist a smile. The pony was a compact, sturdy bay, seemingly unfazed by the activity in the stable yard. Tiny ears pricked, he looked around with interest. He had a kind eye, she noted, and thanked providence Lord Hawke had chosen so well.

Edward's blissful reaction to his pony was a delight to see. "Humbug," he cried, going immediately to the pony's side.

"I will never understand why he persists in calling the pony Humbug," Hawke murmured close to Claudia's ear.

He was too close. She could still smell his shaving soap and the costmary from his shirt. It unnerved her.

"I explained," she managed to say with effort.

"I know, I know," he muttered before going to Edward's side to talk quietly with him regarding his new mount. A fine saddle was brought out. Naturally, nothing would do but that Edward try it out. In a short time he was seated high on the pony's back.

"Look, Mama! I am riding!"

The pony flicked an ear toward the lad, most likely wondering what all the commotion was about.

"Yes, dear. Jem will lead you about in the paddock for a bit. If I know you at all, you will listen to all he says and do so well that you will be riding across the meadow in no time."

Edward gave her a somber nod. "Yes, Mama."

The two men and the boy commenced a low conversation. At least the men talked, the boy politely listened for the most part. That he listened carefully augured well for his future.

Claudia wondered if she dared hobble back to the house. Her stomach was still empty, as she had slept late. Glancing about, she spotted a stick that looked to be about the proper length. She was able to nudge it closer with her good foot. From there it was a simple matter to pick it up and rise. Hopping might be ungraceful. It was effective, however.

At least until she was swept into Hawke's arms and given a small shake. "My dear, do you never learn?"

"I am hungry." She met his gaze and decided that she might have used the wrong words. That look of desire that she had seen flare in his eyes before, returned. It was intense, devouring her. She licked her lips, suddenly nervous—which was nothing new when she was around Lord Hawke.

"I also have a hunger." His reply made her wish she had been more careful in what she said. His grin was too perceptive. Blessedly, he didn't say for *what* he hungered.

"That is, I haven't had any breakfast yet. I long for a cup of tea and a slice of toast with strawberry jam." She gave him an affronted look.

"And I am a heartless grouch. My dear, you should have said something." He looked back over his shoulder, told Jem what was to be done, then marched to the kitchen door and into the house.

In the short time Lord Hawke had been around he had said "my dear" more often than the late Lord Fairfax had in the four years of their marriage. It was most curious. Claudia decided it wouldn't be worth her while to challenge him on the matter. He would think of some utterly wild excuse and she would feel silly.

"Lawks a mercy," Cook exclaimed as Hawke strode through the kitchen and along the hall to the sitting room.

The sofa was a welcome retreat.

"Mrs. Tibbins will have your tea and toast here within minutes." It was easy to see he was accustomed to people doing his bidding without question.

Claudia smiled. There was an "or else" in his voice that she didn't miss and she doubted if her staff did either. "Thank you." She directed the talk away from her. "Edward is thrilled with Humbug. He'll be here before long to properly thank you."

"The three of us will ride out together. I want to observe him ride, and I daresay you will as well." Hawke gave her a steady look, defying her to refuse.

"I haven't ridden in the past year. I found it extremely difficult." It was a complex matter, not easy to explain.

"As a matter of fact you have scarce gone anywhere. You walk a great deal—to the village and neighbors." His gaze bore into her with steady regard, the blue most intimate.

Claudia stiffened. "That is no business of yours, my lord."

"The sooner you get back on a horse the better it will be for you." He gently took her hand in his. His gaze was most persuasive and seemed understanding.

Claudia knew she would be on her gentle mare, come what may. And she was equally certain that this aggravating man would bully her into riding with him and Edward. Well, at least having the boy with them would prevent anything of a romantic nature from occurring. The worst of it all was that she didn't know if she was displeased at that thought or not.

Chapter Five

*C*laudia stretched out in bed and tested her foot, turning it first one way, then the other. She gazed up at the elaborate tester on her four poster bed. Pale almond green silk was gathered to the center and used as lining for the ruffles around the edge. She loved this room with its soft rose walls, elegantly decorated ceiling, and tall windows that looked out onto her gardens. An enormous looking glass hung between the two windows, offering excellent light for her dressing table between them. She had spent quite a few hours on the chintz daybed at the foot of her immense bed that seemed far too large for one.

Not that she missed her husband. She'd not admit the relief she felt at being alone, using the bailiff to manage the estate.

After several days of rest the ankle seemed well enough for her to attend the fête champêtre today. Edward and Olivia were so looking forward to it. It would be a simple matter to sit down whenever her ankle felt weak or began to ache. She knew that Adela would wish to saunter along at a stroll.

After arriving late last evening, throwing the entire household into a quiet tizzy, Adela might possibly be tired. Although she certainly didn't *look* fatigued in the least! Claudia anticipated some good chats with her friend.

Reflecting on the past few days, Claudia couldn't recall when she had been so confused. Lord Hawke had appeared at Fairfax Hall every day, some days remaining for lunch, other times for dinner. He made his concern for her evident in many little ways, yet not so obvious that Olivia had tumbled to his interest. Precisely what his interest might be puzzled Claudia. She had made it clear she wanted no clandestine affair. She might be a widow, but she would not be a scandalous one. If he continued to call her his "dear" she might have to say something, though. Particularly were he to do so while at the fête today. She needed to be extremely cautious. Reputations were such fragile things. Once lost, a reputation was nearly impossible to regain. Suspicion lingered forever.

Mary entered quietly. When the maid saw Claudia was awake she set the pitcher of hot water on the dressing table, then stirred the embers in the fireplace, adding a bit of coal to take the chill from the early morning air. "What wish you to wear this day, my lady?"

"The French gray jaconet, I believe." It was quietly elegant enough for the fête yet not overly fussy. In short order Claudia was prepared to face the day, neatly garbed with a pretty confection of a day cap covering her blond curls. She studied her image in the looking glass on her dressing table.

"Pity you must cover your hair, my lady," Mary ventured to offer while pinning the cap in place. "I should think his lordship would be admiring those curls could he see them."

"I need to be proper, Mary." The thought of Lord Hawke threading his hands through her hair made her swallow rather hard. Really, she must get control of herself. He was disturbing her hard-won peace even when not at her side!

The maid gave her an impish look, then grinned. "I am thinking proper ladies don't have as much fun."

Claudia silently agreed, but bestowed an admonishing look on the maid, one that silenced her immediately.

Mrs. Tibbins was all of a flutter when Claudia confronted her in the entry hall. "Problems, Mrs. Tibbins?"

"It is the village festivity, my lady. With Lady Dunston here, I am in a quandary as to which of the servants may attend." The housekeeper had made it plain that guest or no, the servants expected to attend the modest village entertainment.

"Send them in little groups of two or three at a time. That way they will all have a chance to be there and not miss out on some of the fun, yet we will have staff to deal with the addition of Lady Dunston to the household."

"Very good, my lady," Mrs. Tibbins said with heartfelt appreciation for a touchy problem solved.

"I trust Lady Dunston's maid is seen to? All is well with our guest?" With the housekeeper at her side, Claudia walked toward the breakfast room. It was a relief to note that her ankle gave her only the faintest twinge.

Mrs. Tibbins looked somewhat affronted that Claudia would so much as question the matter. "Indeed, my lady."

Claudia had finished a light breakfast when Adela entered the room. She was garbed in an almond pink sarsenet gown trimmed with deep green riband. The rows of embroidered tucks around the lower edge of the skirt and the cleverly puffed sleeves that had more of the embroidery proclaimed it as coming from London. Claudia might not have gone up to Town but she could recognize a premier mantua-maker's skill when she saw it.

"Tea and toast, my dear," Adela requested nicely. "Then we can begin to catch up on all the news and gossip and the latest in fashions."

"Is it the latest fashion to indulge in handsome footmen?" Claudia teased in a soft voice.

When Adela had stepped from her elegant traveling carriage an incredibly handsome footman had assisted her. Claudia couldn't recall when she had seen a more dashingly virile male . . . unless she included Lord Hawke in her consideration.

Claudia had blinked at this specimen of male beauty before leaving the front door to greet her dear friend.

"I was most impressed, dear Adela," she now murmured to her friend over her morning meal.

"He is striking, is he not?" Adela said quietly in reply. One never knew when a servant might overhear a discussion. "With my husband gone aloft, I have found it delightful to surround myself with splendid young men. And he is all of that."

Putting aside the matter of the awe-inspiring footman, Adela, Lady Dunston, put her hand out to Claudia. "I am so pleased you invited me for a visit. Life was becoming a trifle tedious. I welcome a change."

Claudia cast a hasty glance at her own very ordinary maid as she departed and barely repressed a grin. "Perhaps I should do the same? Only I cannot imagine life tedious with such an Adonis around you."

"Mind you, I did bring him along with me for a reason."

Claudia burst into laughter. "You are truly a wicked woman, my dear friend."

"So I am. Although I must confess all is not as you might think. With those muscles, gentlemen think twice before accosting me when I travel." She exchanged a meaningful look with Claudia. Both women knew the trials of being without male protection.

"Do you have to pay him more to keep him from being lured away from your employ?" Claudia gave her friend a thoughtful look. Perhaps there was something in her reasoning.

"He is satisfied where he is." Adela looked complacent.

Claudia chuckled as intended. "You are just in time to join us in some village festivity. There is to be a fête champêtre today for all to attend." Seeing that her guest had finished her light repast, Claudia led her friend to the drawing room located on the ground level as the more modern houses were designed.

Adela cast a look of astonishment at her friend while walking at her side. "Claudia, tell me you jest. A village fête champêtre? I cannot even imagine such a thing." She settled onto the sofa, draping her skirt in an attractive manner.

"The leading light of our village attended one held by the bishop and his wife and came home with ambitions. I suspect it will be all quite innocent and perhaps a notch above our usual village fair. But it is a diversion and as such is most welcome." Claudia shrugged. "As you just pointed out there are moments when an amusement is most agreeable."

"I do not understand why you persist in remaining buried in the country." Adela gazed about her at the comfortably furnished room and sighed. "It is all well and good to have a lovely home, but there is no challenge here, my dear."

Edward came clattering down the stairs to find his stepmother, then when he saw Lady Dunston stopped at once. "I am happy to see you, ma'am." He executed a neat little bow before giving her a hopeful look.

She turned to summon the handsome footman who had just entered the room with a neatly wrapped parcel. "Here, you wretched boy, I think I know what you might like." She nodded to the footman, who in turn placed the package on the low table near where Edward stood.

Nothing would do but for Edward to immediately sit down and tear off the wrapping of his large package. "Soldiers! A whole army! Even horses and cannons and everything!" he cried as the magnificence of the gift was revealed.

"It ought to keep him occupied for an hour or two," Adela said quietly while she smiled down at the excited boy.

"What a pity you never had any children. They are a comfort when one's husband has gone aloft," Claudia said smiling, although it was faintly bittersweet, for Edward was not her own.

Adela glanced to where the handsome footman stood by the door and murmured, "I have found other comforts, my dear."

What reply might have been made to this shocking comment was not to be heard. A carriage rolled up before the front of the house and within minutes Lord Hawke strolled into the room after having assured Mrs. Tibbins she needn't announce him.

"I see it all now," Adela said with a laugh while Lord Hawke examined Edward's gift. She added in an undertone, "Indeed, there is a challenge, and such a one. Most impressive, dear girl."

"Ah, Lady Dunston." Hawke turned from Edward to bow to the guest. "Claudia said she was expecting you. I trust you will not deny us the pleasure of your company when we attend the local festivity?" He bowed over her hand, then assumed a rather protective stance by Claudia's chair.

She would like to have scolded him for this, but in light of Adela's remarks remained silent.

"I believe it might be far more interesting than I would have thought possible. A village fête champêtre is somewhat beyond my imagination, but it should prove curiously entertaining!" She glanced at her footman, giving him a faint nod of dismissal.

Edward was obviously torn between remaining at home with his wondrous gift and attending the village fair. No one could convince *him* it would be anything other than a fair.

"Edward, fetch your cap," Claudia instructed. "I believe there are to be jesters and a puppet show."

The boy ran at once, clearly entranced with the idea of such rare entertainment. The toys could wait until later since they would not disappear while he was away.

"You plan to remain with Claudia for a time?" Lord Hawke's words were full of speculation.

Claudia turned to see Lord Hawke bestow a narrow-eyed stare on Adela. What on earth was going on? The beautiful Adela never received cold looks or ones implying she wasn't welcome.

"I trust you will not find it too dull in the country," he continued as though convinced otherwise.

Was that a hint of warning in his voice? Claudia scarce knew what to make of his behavior.

"Why does that sound more like a threat instead of a hope?" Adela drifted to the door. "All this to-do made me forget I ought to change if we are to attend this fête in the village. Simon," she said with an artless wave at the footman, who had remained outside the drawing room, "be ready to go with me to this rural jollification."

The footman merely nodded, all six foot plus of him—thick golden hair, liquid brown eyes, and broad smile—ready and waiting in his rich blue livery.

Speechless, Claudia could only stare.

"Did you anticipate Lady Dunston's latest setup?" Lord Hawke said when the footman had left the house and Adela had gone up to her room to don a spencer over her dress.

"Adela is welcome in my home regardless of any notion she may have acquired." Claudia was terribly conscious of the tall man at her side. Quite as virile as the footman and far more polished, not to forget as handsome as may be, he was a threat to any single woman's—or widow's—self-possession. He was the sort of man who lingered in a woman's thoughts long after he had departed. And as to dreams . . . well, it was a very good thing no one could be privy to hers!

"Here I am, ready and waiting," Adela sang out as she whisked into the room where Claudia and Lord Hawke remained in tense silence. She looked from one to the other, shaking her head in mock dismay. "Have I upset you? You look disapproving, Lord Hawke." She adjusted the cuff of her deep rose spencer. Her bonnet was a confection of fine straw and roses.

Before Claudia could think of a plausible reply for the tension in the room, Edward came bounding down the stairs, all enthusiasm. Olivia, garbed in a subtle combination of soft violet muslin with a deep violet spencer over it, sedately followed. A violet reticule dangled from one hand. Her bonnet was a delightful chip straw with violet silk flowers trimming it and tied under her firm chin with a violet riband. Claudia hoped the vicar would be suitably impressed.

In her French gray with its tucked hem and long sleeves that had several rows of gathers, Claudia felt rather prim. She reached up to finger the delicate lace ruff at her neck. Adela's gown had a low neck that decently covered her. Barely. They were both widows, but only Claudia looked the part.

Adela's footman returned to place a shawl tenderly around her shoulders. She gave Lord Hawke an amused glance before turning to Olivia to compliment her on her looks.

"Well," Lord Hawke growled at Claudia, "we had best be on our way."

"All in one carriage, my lord?" Adela said, shooting him an arch look of amazement.

"I suspect we can contrive it if we wish." Apparently Lord Hawke was not to be lured into an exchange on the matter.

With Edward dancing along in impatience and Olivia attempting to explain why they were to have a fête rather than the usual autumn fair, Claudia found herself walking at Lord Hawke's side to where the carriage awaited them. She noted that Adela's footman was now seated up behind with the groom.

"I cannot say I approve of your guest, my dear."

"Isn't it a wonderful thing that your approval is not required, my lord?" Claudia responded cordially. She would not toady to this man, no matter how he affected her.

How he might have retaliated to this challenge was not to be known as the others were scrambling into the carriage. Claudia soon found herself seated cozily by his lordship, with Edward on her other side by the window, peering out as though by such effort he could arrive at the fête that much sooner.

Claudia could feel the heat from his lordship's body. She inhaled deeply, and relished the scent of his lotion. It simply was not fair. He was too enticing! Yet she would not yield her place to Adela. She could look to her own efforts to find a gentleman.

And what popped that thought into her head! A gentleman who interested her? But hadn't she insisted she was content to be alone? Did she not claim to be settled with Edward? Yet an argument from Hawke returned to her. What would happen when Edward went off to school, grew up, married?

The dower house was not a very pleasant place. It would be wise to have it painted and kept in order. Perhaps she could put a few pieces of her favorite furniture there? The house would seem more welcoming.

"And what teases your mind so that you frown, if I may ask, my dear?" Lord Hawke inquired. The noise of the carriage would make it difficult for the others to overhear his intimately spoken words.

"Actually I was thinking of the dower house. It is in shocking disrepair. I ought to do something about it."

"If you like. Although you won't live there, but with your desire to keep things in order for Edward, I expect there is no stopping you." He lightly dismissed her intentions.

He shifted slightly, bringing his thigh firmly against hers. Goodness, but she was far too aware of him. She hoped she wasn't blushing. Blondes with fair skin were so prone to such.

"It is quite warm for August, is it not?" Olivia said.

Thankful for the rescue of sorts, Claudia hastened to reply. "Indeed, it is. I trust there will be lemonade for us at this fête."

"You are wise to bypass the cider. It can be devilishly potent." Lord Hawke looked down at her with an amused expression on his face.

Claudia wondered if the cider could be any more potent than he was. She merely smiled and said nothing.

The coachman reined in near the village green. Adela's footman assisted each woman from the coach, standing at attention for Lord Hawke, and smiling at Edward.

"Lord Fairfax," the vicar caroled to Edward as he crossed the street to welcome them all to the fair. "There is a Punch and Judy on the far side. I feel certain you will be most entertained by it." When Edward had scampered off in that direction, the vicar bowed to Claudia, smiled agreeably to Lord Hawke, but gave the nicely garbed Olivia no more than a nod. When he espied Adela he came up short, staring a moment at the fashionably dressed stranger with her footman closely in attendance. He looked to Claudia, his eyes questioning.

"Lady Dunston, may I present Vicar Woodley?"

To say the vicar was bowled away was to put it mildly. Olivia gave Claudia a tight-lipped smile before leaving the little group to greet one of her friends.

Adela gave her hand to the vicar, but made it clear, at least to Claudia, that she had not the slightest interest in him in any way at all.

"Shall we stroll about the, er, fête?" Lord Hawke took possession of Claudia's hand, tucked it close to his side in the crook of his arm, and proceeded to walk slowly away.

"We simply cannot leave Adela behind," Claudia whispered furiously. "She is my guest!"

His lordship glanced back and chuckled. "The vicar is falling all over himself to be gracious to Lady Dunston. It would be cruel to take her away from him."

"I do not understand you in the least," Claudia complained. Yet she enjoyed her escort. She could see the looks sent his way from all the women they passed.

"Good. See that it remains that way for the present."

"What?" Claudia was totally at sea. This man was beyond infuriating.

A maypole—quite out of season—had been erected on the other side of the green. There was an archery contest for those so inclined. Mrs. Alcock had insisted upon all the servants being dressed up like gardeners, for what possible reason escaped Claudia.

Mrs. Alcock bustled up to Claudia and Lord Hawke. Ignoring his lordship, she bestowed a sweet smile on Claudia. "So nice you could attend our little festivity, dear Lady Fairfax. I trust all is well at the Hall? And you have a guest, I see. How lovely." She paused. "Tell me, are you still painting fairies?"

The question was asked in the same tone she might have used in inquiring if Claudia was still using witchcraft.

"I enjoy painting, Mrs. Alcock." She said nothing about fairies. What she painted was her own business.

"Lady Fairfax is quite gifted in painting flowers, as you might know." Lord Hawke took a step closer to Claudia.

She gave him a sharp look, wondering what the town gossip would make of his behavior. "How kind of you to say so, my lord." Her words revealed nothing more than polite appreciation.

Mrs. Alcock was called away, leaving Claudia to breathe her thanks. "That woman is . . . difficult."

"I say there," came a voice from behind them. "That is you, isn't it, Hawke?" The speaker joined Claudia and Lord Hawke directly. With him were two other very handsome gentlemen.

"Max! I assume you got my letter. Pace and Lodge with you as well? On your way to some hunting up north?"

Claudia thought Lord Hawke did not seem pleased to see his friends. A more offhand welcome she couldn't imagine.

"Hawke, you did invite me," Max reminded. "When we found there was to be a fête in the village today, the others decided to join me." He eyed Claudia with an appreciative smile.

Hawke wished his good friends to Land's End. They were all good-looking, wealthy, and on the lookout for a wife. Not one of them was fit to tie Claudia's slipper. She wouldn't know that, of course. Why had he invited Max, of all men!

"Lady Fairfax, may I present Max—Lord Elliot, Lord Pace, and Mr. Lodge. I went to school with them and we have known each other for ages." The words were a dry concession.

Claudia murmured her acknowledgments of their elegant bows, each one taking hold of her hand in a friendly manner.

Hawke kept her close to his side. If these dunderheads had any brains at all, they would understand his position.

"I say, old chap, would it be imposing if these chaps racked up with you as well?" The brashness of the query was lessened by a jaunty smile from Elliot.

Accepting the inevitable, Hawke agreed graciously. "I've rooms to spare. You are most welcome."

Lady Dunston drifted up to join them, beaming a charming smile. "Hello! How nice to see you all again. Did I hear you intend to remain here for a bit? Splendid!"

The three men eyed her and Claudia, then nodded eagerly. "We wouldn't miss *your* company, dear ladies."

Hawke felt prickles of unease creep up his spine.

Chapter Six

"*M*ax." Hawke turned to his old friend, Maximillian, Viscount Elliot. "I am surprised to see you so soon." Hawke knew his voice had an edge to it, but that couldn't be helped. The last thing he needed or wanted at this point were three handsome, wealthy single gentlemen around. Claudia would appeal to any of them. He liked Max, but not as a rival.

"Your mysterious disappearance from town brought us all here out of curiosity. And you *did* invite me." Max cast a look at Lady Fairfax and gave Hawke the grin the ladies termed devastating. "All is explained now."

He felt like growling at his crony. "You may be the next thing to a brother, Max, but there are times when I prefer to do my hunting alone." Hawke glanced back to where Claudia stood chatting with several women. Mrs. Alcock appeared to be controlling the conversation. Judging from the expression on Claudia's face, it was not an agreeable experience. A few more minutes and he would step in to rescue her.

Max ambled along the green at Hawke's side, absently tapping his leg with his crop. "Things changed since you wrote? Sorry about the others; they insisted upon tagging along. But a little diversion never hurt. We could, ah, keep the other ladies occupied so to give you free rein."

"Miss Greene is mad for the vicar. I doubt she will offer you the time of day." Hawke grimaced at the thought of the vicar, who only had eyes for Claudia, and Olivia Greene, who had a hopeless passion for the vicar.

After a hasty glance back at the woman under discussion, Max chuckled. "A bit of competition is often what a reluctant swain needs."

"She is a nice person. I'd not want to see her hurt." Hawke knew what he'd said was true. Olivia was kind and gentle, the perfect mate for a vicar. He didn't see it, his eyes on Claudia. Or was it that he saw himself moving into Fairfax Hall, with access to the fortune Claudia received as her jointure?

"And Lady Dunston? The widow left Town in a flurry. I heard it had to do with visiting a sick friend. Lady Fairfax looks to be in uncommonly fine health. Is Lady Dunston also out of our range? That would be a cruel blow!" He cast a look toward that lady, his brows raised in question.

"That is for the lady to decide. All I say is to bridle your charm when it comes to Lady Fairfax. I saw her first. She is mine."

Hawke couldn't believe what he had just said. Had he really stated his intentions so firmly? With a warning glance at Max and a hope he might convey the idea to their mutual friends, Hawke returned to take Claudia's arm, once again tucking it close to his side. She had been stoically listening to that officious woman who had criticized painting fairies. Hawke thought she had endured quite enough of that woman's spite.

"You seem surprised to see your friends." Claudia clung to his arm in a satisfying way. Perhaps she was glad to be rescued?

"I am. What was that dreadful woman saying to you just now? I can feel your ruffled feathers." Hawke studied the exquisite face of the woman at his side, wondering for the hundredth time how the late Lord Fairfax could have preferred the highly dubious charms of Mrs. Norton to his beautiful wife.

"It seems she takes exception to what I paint. She's not afraid to express her disapproval. I fully expected her to summon the vicar to add his weight to her argument." There was no doubt Claudia felt upset, brief though the exchange was.

"I have yet to view your finished paintings, my dear, but I venture to say they are as lovely as you. What is wrong with painting fairies, may I ask? I can see no harm in that." Hawke guided Claudia some distance apart from Lady Dunston and Olivia Greene. He sensed that whatever reply he might be given, it would be a trifle more open were she not overheard by anyone, least of all her friends.

"She insists they are heathen nonsense." Claudia's indignation was almost amusing, but he could sympathize with her feelings. It was none of that old harridan's business what Claudia did with her time and talent. "Her daughter is her echo, a most annoying trait! I believe she rather fancies you, if you must know. That might account for her mother trying to discredit me in the eyes of the community . . . and your eyes as well."

It was a pity he couldn't send the tartar off to stay with the bishop permanently. She could not be allowed to harass Claudia. He patted Claudia's hand, ignoring what anyone might think of his actions. Surely his approval would count for more than Mrs. Alcock! He considered how he might console Claudia.

"I have seen a few of your flower sketches. You must show me some of your charming fairies. I would see for myself what that battle-ax thinks depraved." Claudia's chuckle was ample reward for his concern. It warmed him, made him long to do more than vanquish an ill-tempered woman from Claudia's path.

Edward dashed up at that moment to ask his stepmother if he might help with the maypole. Given permission, he ran happily off to where a group of boys and girls gathered about the tall pole near the center of the green. One by one each child clutched a bright colored ribbon. It was Olivia who sorted them all out, arranging the girls in the inner circle, the boys in the outer circle. She summoned a slim fellow standing nearby. Within moments the chap started to play his flute and the children began the complicated dance, weaving about the pole.

It always amazed Hawke that the young ones enjoyed the activity so much. This group was particularly adept, not getting ribands tangled, not falling down or pushing into one another. Perhaps that strangers viewed their game made a difference? At any rate, it was a colorful display.

"Edward does handsomely well, dear Claudia," Lady Dunston said as she joined them, Max at her side. That he paid far more attention to the lovely widow than to the antics of those at the maypole didn't seem to bother her.

"Yes, he does, doesn't he?" Claudia replied with a fond look at her stepson. He, in turn, danced about the pole with a determined expression on his face. It was clear he was not going to make a misstep if he could help it. While the maypole dancing was traditionally the province of girls, there was a shortage of girls round about, which led to boys being included— to Edward's satisfaction. They were to be given treats following, and that probably accounted for much of his enthusiasm.

At last the somewhat complex dance concluded. Olivia handed out sweets to all those who had joined in the fun. The vicar paid her a polite compliment for the success of her efforts, but scarce noticed her blushing acceptance of his words. She gazed after him, a crushed expression briefly crossing her face.

"He truly is a clod, I believe," Hawke said to Claudia for her ears alone. "Or perhaps merely blind."

"He fancies to fix his attention on me, I fear." She darted a rosy-cheeked look at Hawke, plainly embarrassed. "I do all I can to discourage him."

"I am certain you would do nothing to hurt Miss Greene's feelings. Perhaps my friends can influence him if they extend their admittedly polished attentions to her. As Max just said to me, there is nothing like a bit of competition to alert a man to the worthiness of a lady."

Her lips quirked in the semblance of a smile. "Perhaps."

"Tell me, is there to be dancing in the tent put up on the far side of the green?" Hawke thought it prudent to change the subject. He didn't want her to question too closely why Max had uttered those words.

"I believe the vicar suggested it to Mrs. Alcock and she most eagerly agreed. The flautist is one of the musicians to play. There are others who will join him later on, I suppose. I fear I am not privy to many of Mrs. Alcock's plans."

"The woman appears to resent you. Or perhaps she is merely jealous of your beauty. You far outshine her daughter, who will likely have her mother's girth before too many years pass." Hawke enjoyed the repeat of that rose tinge on Claudia's cheeks. She could have no idea how the color enhanced her fragile blond beauty. Her eyes flashed with rebuke at his words. Their blue depths became deeper, like a storm-darkened sea, when she became angry or annoyed.

"What utter nonsense, my Lord Hawke. Mrs. Alcock is a handsome woman, well liked in the village. Her daughter is often engaged in worthy tasks." Claudia pursed her lips in a prim line, giving him another chastising look. Amusement lurked in her eyes, however, negating the effect of her words.

"Her mama does not like you, my dear. That is obvious." He let the matter drop, seeing that it made Claudia uncomfortable.

Max and Lady Dunston joined them again. Max looked about them, seeming to catch sight of the archery butt that had been set up. He tilted his head to challenge Hawke. "Archery? I believe I trounced you the last time we contended."

Not wanting to back down at the teasing grin on Max's face, Hawke nodded. Keeping Claudia close to his side, he followed Max and Lady Dunston to where the archery butt stood. He most likely hadn't held a bow and arrow in his hands since Max had last challenged him to a contest. He very much doubted if he had improved in the interim.

"I ought to have a kiss for luck," he murmured to Claudia, more to see the faint rose tinge on her cheeks rather than actually believing she might assent. He suspected he had not improved her opinion of him when he had stupidly accused her of kissing like a spinster. Her late husband had truly lacked in teaching his young wife the delights of marriage. It hadn't helped that Hawke had called attention to her insufficiency. Just because he wanted to correct the lack was no reason for him to upbraid her—or kiss her as he had. The temptation had proven beyond his ability to resist.

With a mischievous sparkle in her eyes, she stretched up to plant a hasty kiss on his cheek, surprising him and most likely everyone around. Not that many people were there, the various attractions drawing people to them.

Mrs. Alcock saw, however. Hawke caught sight of her staring at Claudia and him, her mouth slack in outrage, her affront plain. What the plump harridan might do as a result worried him. Claudia was so careful of her reputation, worried that any transgression might affect her stepson as well as her standing in the community. Still, what had been done was done. He would rectify matters should it become necessary.

"I cannot lose," Hawke declared to Max, a surprisingly confident feeling coming over him. Could that kiss possibly work some magic? He knew that Claudia certainly had a powerful effect on him.

Claudia watched each man select a bow, then arrows, arguing good-naturedly between them. Her heart pounded in her chest while she wondered if she might sink through the grass. Had she actually dared to offer Lord Hawke a quick kiss while in the middle of the green with everyone in the surrounding area likely watching? She noted the thunderous expression that sat on the vicar's face. It gave him the aspect of an irate bulldog.

He crossed to meet Mrs. Alcock, the pair of them looking as though they had been eating lemons. They immediately began a confidential conversation. And they gazed at her with narrowed eyes. The vicar was likely scandalized. Heaven only knew what Mrs. Alcock might do or say. She could stir up the women if she chose. What possible danger could result from a quick peck on a cheek was above Claudia.

She tried to shake off the feeling of impending doom, resolutely turning her attention to the archery contest.

"You go first, Max. Since you won the last time, I think that gives me a bit of leverage here." Lord Hawke gave his friend a shrewd look.

Claudia glanced sideways at Lord Hawke. He appeared so confident, so very assured of himself. Would that she could overcome her own shyness, her fear of censure. True, it was more for Edward's sake than her own, but the disapproval of the local women would be an ordeal she could well do without.

It would not be pleasant to withdraw from what little contact she had with the surrounding society. They were a close-knit group, treating her like an outsider from the day she had arrived at Fairfax Hall. They had not wasted any time to drop little hints about her husband's infidelity. Oh, no, they had taken righteous pride in letting her know what manner of man she had married—quite as though she might alter the situation!

Still, it would be hard for Olivia and Edward were she to become persona non grata in the village. She didn't know how to tell Lord Hawke that his interest in her was dangerous, that the locals would take great delight in painting the widow with a tarry brush. They were always polite to her face. She had trusted them at first—until she learned what sort of people they were. How different they behaved from the people in her home village. But there, her father was rector and his family accorded a certain amount of deference. Here, she was merely the widow of a wealthy baron who had also been most unfaithful and had left several children on Mrs. Norton in the next village.

Her gloomy thoughts were broken off when Lord Elliot scored quite well in the contest. Lord Hawke stepped forward, bow and arrow in hand.

"It is impossible to shoot with this cursed coat on," he muttered. "Here . . ." He dropped the bow and arrow on the ground, then peeled off his coat, handing it to Claudia with a pleading look on his handsome face.

She accepted his coat, totally unable to utter a word. The fine cambric linen shirt could not conceal his trim, yet quite muscular torso. While she had glimpsed her late husband's form more than once, it bore the faintest resemblance to what was on display before her eyes now. It explained why she never saw a gentleman without his coat. The sight was too arousing by far.

As she watched he drew the bow back, nocked the arrow with care, held it up before him, and took aim. She held her breath, not wishing to break his concentration in any way.

Dead-center hit!

"Bravo! I should say that was a winner!" she exclaimed, for once not caring who heard what she said.

"I said you would bring me luck." His eyes met her gaze, holding warmth that caused her heart to accelerate. What message he sent was undecipherable.

She swallowed with care, her misgivings creeping up again. He would tease and torment her, then disappear as he had after her late husband's funeral. With a start, she realized she had turned to Lord Hawke in blind reliance, needing his calm acceptance of the situation to survive. It had not been easy to ignore the knowing looks of those who had attended the funeral.

Where her husband had been prior to the accident was common knowledge. He was returning home from seeing Mrs. Norton. Claudia had felt so humiliated. Yet she had managed to hold her head high, ignoring the speculative looks, the pious platitudes that had rained down on her head.

After all, she had the Hall and her stepson, not to forget the wealth she now controlled. But she missed the companionship of other women, the little teas and card parties that were a large part of country society. There was utterly nothing she could do to change their perception of her. It appeared her role as the forsaken wife of an important man would haunt her all her days. It was not as dire as being divorced, but it was a long way from being accepted.

The men did three rounds total with the bows and arrows. Lord Hawke won twice, Lord Elliot once.

Lord Hawke turned to her, a triumphant grin on his face that took away the alarming aspect of his appearance. It made him seem far less dangerous than she knew him to be.

He assumed that she would help him shrug into his coat. He slipped it on, waiting for her to smooth it over his shoulders, to adjust it properly which she did with misgivings.

The feelings that tore through her when she touched his body—even through the thickness of the fine Bath cloth—should not happen. He was merely a neighbor. And she was nothing more than an idiot!

"I hear music." Lord Hawke turned to face her, again taking her hand to place it on his arm in such a way that she was very close to his side. Dangerous, that is what he was.

"They must be ready to begin the dancing," Adela cried with pleasure. "Come, we must join in the dance." She led Lord Elliot to the vast tent where the musicians played a bit of music to alert those attending the fête. Olivia and the two men followed.

Claudia sensed when Lord Hawke looked down at her. She met his gaze briefly, then flicked her attention to the tent ahead of them. "I suppose we must go as well."

"Do you not enjoy dancing?" He kept her close to him, most likely because of the press of bodies as they thronged into the gaily colored tent.

"I have had little opportunity to dance these past years, my lord. I did," she said with a faint sigh, "before I married."

They stood to one side while a country-dance began, watching the line form, then re-form as the people went through the complicated pattern of the dance. When Lord Hawke excused himself, Claudia felt alone, vulnerable.

"Max," Hawke said, nodding to his friend, "I need to speak to someone. Will you guard Lady Fairfax while I do?" At the answering nod, he disappeared toward the other end of the tent.

He wasn't gone long. Within minutes he returned, looking most satisfied with himself. After thanking his friend, he again placed Claudia's hand on his arm while they listened to the music and watched the dancers.

At last the country-dance concluded. Those who

had participated strolled about the perimeter of the tent, chatting and exchanging words with friends.

The musicians didn't wait long before the next dance.

"They are playing a waltz!" Adela exclaimed. "Oh, I adore waltzing. You know how, Claudia. Can you resist?"

The sight of Mrs. Alcock frowning in her direction made Claudia firm her lips. It seemed that regardless of what she did to appease the lady, there was no pleasing her. Claudia looked up to see Lord Hawke watching her. "I cannot deny it appeals. The music is irresistible, too tempting for me to withstand."

He held out his arm and swept her into a loose embrace, such as was proper in a waltz. Only, she had never experienced a waltz like this. His guidance was skillful, he spoke not a word to tease her, but as they moved through the steps of the dance he drew her into contact with his form. *That* was what sent heat through her, scorched her nerves.

"You perform the waltz very well, my dear." Hawke shifted his hand on her back, bringing her a trifle closer to him.

"You do as well, although I daresay Mrs. Alcock thinks you border on the scandalous."

"Does what she thinks matter so much to you?" He deftly swung her around to avoid another couple.

"I am not sure anymore. It did. Perhaps I should do as I please without regard to what she or anyone else might think. I believe I have become rather tired of her narrow precepts." She considered the matter a moment, then continued. "I may need to find someone other than the vicar to school Edward in his Latin as well. But Olivia would be unhappy in that event, so perhaps I must continue to deal with him as best I can."

She looked up to see if Lord Hawke comprehended the extent of her dilemma. It was difficult to think well, for his nearness rather scrambled her brains, turning them to mush.

"There are a number of solutions to your problem."

She waited to hear what those might be. His lordship was strangely silent, however. "And?" she prodded.

"You will learn in due time."

"That is no answer!" she declared in a huff.

He chuckled, a rich, deep sound of amusement. "Your ankle is quite healed. I will come over in the morning and we can take that ride with Edward. I shall even bring a suitable mount for you, my dear. I think that slug in the stable that you intend to ride not worth its oats. I mean to tutor Edward, and you if necessary, in riding."

"I am not very good. I'll be the first to tell you that. Fairfax was forever telling me that I was hopeless in the saddle." She compressed her lips, recalling that her late husband found her hopeless in everything but caring for his son.

"Considering your grace otherwise, I suspect he was an inept instructor. I am a gifted teacher, my dear."

"I'm not, you know." At his raised brow she added, "Your dear. I belong to no one."

He made no reply to her challenging remark but merely smiled in that enigmatic way he had that told her absolutely nothing.

The waltz ended and they joined Lord Elliot and Adela near the entrance to the tent.

"I suggest we leave," Adela said with a saucy smile at Lord Elliot. "Tea at your house, Claudia?"

"By all means." She turned to Lord Hawke. "I imagine your friends will wish to transfer their things to your home?"

"I fancy they have that well in hand. Max, you, Pace, and Lodge bring your things along and follow us to Fairfax Hall."

"With great pleasure. I see them over there, flirting with a couple of the local ladies." Lord Eliot murmured something to Adela before striding across the green to his friends.

"Gather up Edward and Olivia, and we'll be on our way."

For once Claudia didn't argue. She couldn't wait to leave.

Chapter Seven

With mixed feelings, Claudia entered the carriage to return to Fairfax Hall. She had behaved quite out of character in her spontaneous kiss on the viscount's cheek. Good heavens, what on earth had come over her? She wasn't even sure she liked the man. Yet the touch had been sweet. She liked the lotion he used. He always smelled good, unlike her late husband. She ignored the little flurry of nerves that swept through her when her lips touched his cheek. It was best not to dwell on that.

The waltz with him had sealed the disapproval from the vicar and Mrs. Alcock. But did she truly care? It seemed as though nothing would ever permit her to attain their good graces. Why bother?

Because, a small voice replied, *you were raised to care. Your parents taught you to be respectable.* And it had hurt very deeply when her late husband had behaved in such a censurable manner. Never would she forget the barely disguised glee in the voice of the woman who let slip the information regarding Mrs. Norton and her four daughters. The words had been accompanied by a pitying look and a studied gaze at Claudia's very slim figure. No sign of offering more children to the baron. Never mind that he rarely sought her bed. No, he had given two more girls to that widow after his marriage to Claudia. It was more than she had ever expected to endure.

Sending Lord Hawke a wary glance, she graciously slid over to allow her nemesis room. Lord Hawke spoke briefly to his friends, then joined the group in the carriage.

"I did not get to ride a donkey," Edward observed sadly.

"I am very proud of you, though. You didn't throw a tantrum like some little children might," Lord Hawke said. He turned to where Claudia nestled in her corner of the carriage. "Would you not say that merited something special?"

"Indeed, it must. You are going riding tomorrow. Perhaps a special treat this evening?" Claudia said in her warmest manner, far too conscious of Lord Hawke's proximity.

"May I stay up late and have a treacle tart? I saw Cook making some this morning."

"That seems likely," Claudia agreed. She turned to Lord Hawke. "You invited Lord Elliot to visit you?"

"Yes. I had no idea he would bring Pace and Lodge with him. They are agreeable chaps, however. You shan't mind them around."

"I met Lord Pace in London," Adela mused. "I believe Mr. Lodge was with him. Is he not the heir to the Earl of Loxley?"

"You have the right of it, Lady Dunston. He's considered a prime catch, especially since Loxley *will* ride hell-for-leather over the moors when hunting." A tinge of amusement colored his voice. He glanced at Claudia, probably noting her prim mouth.

"Hawke, your language," Claudia murmured, hoping he could hear her over the noise of the carriage.

"Sorry, my dear. Hard to know how else to describe him. Loxley is so hunting mad, the odds on his survival are poor."

"Hmm. Perhaps we ought to invite the Alcock's daughter to meet Mr. Lodge." Adela gave them a mischievous smile. "At least she is not all airs and graces like her mother."

"Lady Dunston, he may seem all ears but he has a proper heart and I believe he deserves a fine lady," Lord Hawke said, his voice amused, a half smile hovering.

Claudia compressed her lips at the apt description of the quiet Mr. Lodge. His ears did stick straight out from his head. Perhaps were he to wear his hair a trifle longer it might help.

"And Lord Pace? What can you tell us about him?" Adela queried, her curiosity odd for a woman who claimed to have no intention of remarrying.

"Nothing much, other than he is a decent chap and quite wealthy. In fact, all three of my friends are well to grass and most likely in the market for a wife, I suspect."

Claudia looked closely at Lord Hawke. It almost seemed he was goaded into his reply. Did he believe that Adela and she were hunting for husbands? She wasn't positive about her friend, but she wasn't.

"What a pity Claudia and I are not in the market for husbands," Adela drawled. "Of course, Olivia is single and I trust heart-whole." She turned to stare at Olivia, who in turn blossomed a lovely shade of pink. "You wouldn't mind being a countess or a baroness, would you, dear girl?"

"What utter rubbish," Olivia declared, astonishing Claudia with her firmness. "I will contrive to be polite to them, nothing more. Poor Mr. Lodge, it is not easy to be so afflicted. He seems nice, though." Olivia assumed a thoughtful expression.

Edward had been nose to the window, gazing at the passing scenery as though he hadn't seen it dozens of times. He looked back to the other passengers. "I hope Cook and Mrs. Tibbins have a splendid tea set out for us—with treacle tarts, too."

That remark, and turning into the drive that led to Fairfax Hall, ended all speculation regarding Olivia and the gentlemen.

They strolled into the house together: Adela and Lord Elliot followed by her footman, then Mr. Lodge, and a very shy Olivia. Lord Pace joined them. Claudia moved to enter the house when Lord Hawke detained her.

"Is Jem Groom the only male around this place? Other than the young stable hands?" Hawke looked concerned. "They are scarce able to defend anyone."

"My late husband's valet left after the funeral, as did the footmen. I haven't bothered to hire replacements. It will be some years before Edward requires a valet." Claudia gave him an amused look, keeping a careful distance from him.

"You need at least one footman, perhaps a butler."

"I have the bailiff to tend the business of running the estate. The others are not necessary." She omitted the time she spent with the bailiff discussing what was to be planned for the coming months. She was quite certain that Lord Hawke would consider her excursions into agriculture so much nonsense. Yet both she and the bailiff were well satisfied with the results.

"I think not. I am uneasy with so little protection for you. This house is laughably easy for a man to enter at any time. The windows open to the touch. The lock on the door is a mere nothing. I would not see, er, Edward harmed."

Claudia grimaced. Of course he was thinking of his ward. Why should he worry about her? "I will consider it, my lord. Now shall we join the others? As hostess it behooves me to pour the tea. Besides, my ankle is wanting me to sit down." Actually, she wasn't in any great pain. It ached just a little.

He became all consideration, ushering her into the house and the large drawing room where the others waited. While the day was pleasant, a small fire smoldered in the grate, taking any chill from the room. Claudia had found that unheated rooms tended to be chilly unless it had turned very hot outside.

Guiding her to a chair, Hawke gently, but firmly, eased her down. "Her ankle is bothering her." He found a footstool and moved it so her foot might rest on it. She was thankful that he did not improperly place her foot *on* the stool. She had behaved in an unseemly fashion quite enough for one day.

"A good cup of tea will ease the pain, I vow," Olivia said earnestly.

Mr. Lodge engaged Olivia in a discussion on the merits of tea, their two heads close together in eager conversation.

Adela informed Mrs. Tibbins of the desire for an ample repast. "We returned early, as you can see. Lady Fairfax has some pain in her ankle. Olivia says tea will help."

Mrs. Tibbins paused at the open door, assessing the cluster of gentlemen and the three ladies. "Vast quantities, I'll be bound," she said with a nod before bustling off to the kitchen.

Lord Elliot proved to be an entertaining guest. He related amusing tales of the *ton* with a kind tongue. Mr. Lodge turned out to be an expert on soldiering, showing an enchanted Edward how to arrange his new soldiers, cannon, and even sketched a scene that could be used as a background. Lord Pace good-naturedly added his thoughts on the matter.

"Your friends are very welcome. It is nice to have such agreeable guests who set out to please. We shall have to think of suitable diversions for them," Claudia murmured to Lord Hawke under the flurry of serving tea. "I ought to be able to think of two young women who would prove agreeable."

"Perhaps only one will be needed," he said with a thoughtful look to where Olivia watched Mr. Lodge and the army.

As the tea arrived, the men left Edward's soldiers to him. Tea was always a welcome pastime.

The maid passed the ample tray of seed cakes, sandwiches, ginger biscuits, and treacle tarts while Claudia poured tea into the delicate cups she had painted with an array of flowers.

"No fairies on these, I see," Hawke teased.

"I have yet to transfer my latest designs to china. First I must paint Edward's dragon for him." She looked to her stepson, pleased that he was arranging his new soldiers on a table to the far side of the room. He had bloomed with the attention from the two gentlemen.

"You do not mind that he plays on that fine table?" Hawke inquired with a faint frown. "I can see he benefits from male companionship."

"The table can be polished again. He will want to take his soldiers up to his room later. For now, it is splendid that he has someone who shows an interest in what he does."

Dismissing the matter of his ward, Hawke looked at Mrs. Tibbins and the maid, his frown deepening. "Lady Dunston has her footman with her. Obviously she sees the need for protection. Why don't you?" He set his cup down with a click, turning to gaze at Claudia with a belligerent expression on his face.

Claudia was surprised at his insistence. "You mentioned that earlier. I see no need . . ."

He broke in to refute her denial. "There is every need. I have a good footman I will send over. He is well trained and is able to provide protection should it be needed."

"I thank you . . . I guess. I confess I had not thought of requiring such." That wasn't quite true. Claudia realized that she ought to have a shield of some sort, if nothing more than something to protect her heart against Lord Hawke. He had not been here long and it seemed to her that he had taken over at her home as well as his. Edward adored him, Olivia deferred to him, Adela flirted with him, and Mrs. Tibbins behaved as though he walked on water.

Quite naturally, he wished his ward to be safe. Although precisely who might do Edward harm she couldn't imagine. The man who stood to inherit the barony should Edward die without issue was presently in Canada. Remote, indeed. Hardly a threat. She had learned that he was pleased with his life there and had no intention of returning to England.

Her mind wandered to the man so near to where she perched on her chair, her foot elevated. Again she wondered why he had come into the country. It was plain that his milieu was in Society—his clothes, his manners, everything about him fairly shouted his position. Did he have an interest in any particular women? She studied him with an oblique look, hoping to do so in such a way that he wouldn't catch her at it. Why did he have to be so dratted handsome? And polished? And kind? It didn't make life any easier for her.

He spent time with friends, but not family—although most of them were rather distant. Was he lonely? Could that explain why he bothered so with Edward, and, incidentally, her? Was that why he had invited a friend to visit? Because his life was dull while in the country?

Well, wasn't that why she had invited Adela to stay? More or less, that is, thinking she would be a barrier against too frequent calls from her neighbor? What a lot of nonsense that was. He came over regardless. And brought others to boot.

"I think your ankle has taken a turn for the worse. You have a rather serious expression on your face. Are you pretending to be better?" Lord Hawke gave her a worried look.

Startled by his question, she shook her head. "Not in the least."

"Nevertheless, I believe we shall go now. I shall be over in the morning to take Edward and you for that ride. You won't forget?"

"I wouldn't be allowed to forget. Edward will be at my bedside first thing in the morning, insisting I rise and dress."

She saw it again, that flicker of desire that had flared in his eyes before. It gave her a strange feeling, a tremor that twinkled down her spine to settle somewhere in her lower regions. She checked her wayward thoughts at once.

He rose, briskly enjoining his friends to depart. "We have tomorrow ahead, and I've no doubt Lady Fairfax would welcome a rest on her bed. Her ankle, you recall." Without adding a word to that, he turned, gathered her up in his arms, and marched up the stairs to her bedroom.

"Rest. I want you along tomorrow, my dear." He paused to gaze about the room. "Perhaps you can have your dinner on a tray? This is a pleasant room. I can see why you enjoy it."

Claudia was most thankful it was as neat as a pin. "Until tomorrow," she managed to say now that she had her breath again. He tended to take it away at times—like when he gathered her close to him. She might have suspected him of deliberately cradling her in his arms, taking his time with reaching her room, but that would have been a lot of nonsense.

Yet when he had gone, silently closing the door behind him, she felt oddly bereft. And if that wasn't the silliest thing she didn't know what was.

Adela poked her head in later. When she saw Claudia was awake, head propped on a fat pillow and foot tenderly cocooned under a light blanket, she entered.

"This has been a most interesting day. I am so glad I decided to accept your invitation. I had thought I might enjoy that footman, but it would never do. I know that now." She twiddled with a fringe on a cushion. In an overly casual voice she continued. "Lord Elliot seems rather nice. He is quite handsome. Good manners."

"Kind to old ladies and no doubt generous to a fault," Claudia added with a chuckle. "How good that he is wealthy. A woman—or widow—wouldn't have to think he courted her for her money. And to think he is in want of a wife! Interesting."

Adela picked up the pillow and tossed it at Claudia, taking a deep breath as she did. "I might know that you would see through me. Don't think I am totally unaware of your feelings, my girl. I can see more than you think."

"How can you be? I am not aware of them myself."

Adela gave her a skeptical look. "Tomorrow Lord Hawke will be here to take you and Edward riding. I shall do my poor best to entertain the other men . . . or shall we all go riding together?"

Claudia sighed. "I expect that would be a very wise notion. Indeed, we shall all go for a ride—even Olivia. I am sure that there is a horse in the stables that will suit you very well. Olivia will be satisfied with the mare Lord Hawke calls a slug. She is an indifferent rider. Lord Hawke said he will bring a mount for me. The gentlemen will have their own horses. We need another woman. Unless you want to explore possibilities with all of them? The three, that is?"

Adela opened the door to the hall, pausing to say, "I note you do not include Lord Hawke in your offer. One is sufficient for me, dearest Claudia. I will ask Olivia who might be a proper addition to our party. We can send an invitation immediately."

The door shut without the revelation as to which one Adela preferred. Claudia thought she knew.

The morning brought a gentle breeze and late summer warmth. Olivia had suggested they invite Miss Dorothy Cork to join the riding party. She had quickly accepted, promising to be at Fairfax Hall early in the day.

Directly following breakfast, Miss Cork came, quite desirous of meeting the strangers. When they arrived, Olivia introduced her to them all. That she left her in the care of Lord Pace was something not missed by Claudia.

"I see Olivia is matchmaking," Lord Hawke said quietly.

Claudia started, unaware he had come so close to her side. "I believe she may decide to ignore the vicar for someone more interested in her. The vicar scarce gives her the time of day. Mr. Lodge is willing to discuss the benefits of tea. That is a vast improvement. Miss Cork is a mild creature, but a pretty one, and kind."

"As are you, my dear . . . usually." He ignored her look of vexation to draw her along with him to where a fine-looking mare stood by his own horse. "This is the animal you are to ride today. I see you have assigned that slug to Olivia. Do you dislike her that much? Unworthy of you, my dear."

"Olivia is but a fair horsewoman. She would not thank me for giving her some mettlesome beast."

"Folly is a gentle mare, quite right for you." He tossed her up on the saddle, standing by while she arranged the skirt of her sensible navy habit and took the reins in hand.

Claudia frowned. "Folly? I do not recall any mention of the horse before." She gave her escort a puzzled look.

Hawke maintained a bland expression. Not for the world would he reveal his purchase of the mare at Tattersall's specifically for Claudia's use. He knew she hadn't bought any horses, nor did she ride much. He believed that Folly would be just the thing for her now. "I was unaware that you were so well acquainted with my stables. Should I be flattered?"

He enjoyed her blush. She was becoming easier for him to read. Not that he minded studying her in the least. It was an occupation he could tell might take years to accomplish.

In short order they were all up and mounted, with Edward riding Humbug between Claudia on Folly and Hawke on Kismet.

"What an odd name for your horse—Kismet." Claudia looked at him as though he was short a sheet to think of such.

"When I first saw him, I knew I'd met my fate, hence the name." To Edward he explained, "Kismet means fate in Turkish."

Edward was busy concentrating on his pony and trying to ape the casual elegance of Lord Hawke on his horse. He merely nodded, confining all thoughts to himself.

"And Folly?" Claudia added with a sly look of amusement on her face.

"Ah, that I can't explain, my dear. Perhaps someday." Hawke knew that his aspirations might amount to no more than folly, resulting in the name. Only time would tell if he succeeded.

"Well, I cannot see what is so secret about a name for a horse," she replied with a touch of pique.

Hawke merely chuckled, then watched Edward for a time before offering him a few tips on coping with his pony.

Miss Cork proved to be adept on horseback, a thing Lord Pace commended. He rode along at her side, quite amiable in his attentions.

Olivia and Mr. Lodge found they suited very well. Olivia lost some of her shyness, chattering to the gentleman with a newfound charm.

"A pity the vicar cannot see her now," Claudia observed to Hawke. "He might welcome her and her ample legacy."

"I predict that the vicar will court and win the Alcock's daughter. He is an ambitious cleric. Mrs. Alcock is not only related to an earl, but to a bishop—hence all her airs and graces, not to forget her ambitions."

"Gracious, I'd not considered that. I am more determined than ever to find someone else to tutor Edward in his Latin."

Hawke watched as she bestowed a fond look on her stepson. Could he persuade her to have Edward's abilities tested by an outsider? If a man could gauge the level of the boy's schooling, perhaps Claudia could be convinced that it would be in the lad's interest to join other schoolboys?

"Edward is doing well with his new pony."

"You chose well when you selected Humbug, my lord. The pair of them are well matched." She bestowed a tentative smile on him. That smile gave rise to hopes.

"For the present. When the lad goes off to Eton, the pony will remain here." Hawke encouraged the boy to trot ahead so he might observe his seat.

"And you are so certain he will go soon?" she said, guarding her words with care.

"Perhaps. Look: he sits so straight, holds the reins well, and shows no reluctance to do what he is told."

Claudia straightened from where she had ever so slightly slumped in the sidesaddle.

"You are doing well this morning, my dear. I think that perhaps Folly will remain in your stables so that you might feel more inclined to ride. Olivia can have the slug. That way you will have company even when I am not to hand."

"I do not require your company in order to ride, Lord Hawke." She tilted her head, casting him a mischievous look. "But it will do Olivia good to get a bit of exercise. Although, I must say that I do not think Mr. Lodge minds her plumpness."

"She is plump; he has ears." Hawke drew a deep

breath. "You never know what will attract one person to another, do you?"

Claudia ignored this. "I ordered a picnic nuncheon to be brought for our pleasure." She pointed her crop in the vague direction of a distant meadow where a pretty little stream wandered through it. Cattle grazed on the far side. The servants, including the footman he had assigned to Fairfax Hall, would be setting forth a feast on the near side of the meadow. "I think we will enjoy it."

Hawke glanced at her. "I am certain of it, my dear." He checked on his friends. They all looked most content with their companions, as he was with Claudia.

Chapter Eight

*H*awke knew that there was nothing to do but accept the picnic, and the company, with good grace. At least the vicar and Mrs. Alcock's plain daughter were not inflicted on them. She might be related to some peer—he couldn't recall which one at the moment—but she had not been blessed with beauty! If she had any other graces, he was unaware of it.

"Oh, how lovely," Miss Cork cried to the group as they set forth. "Not a cloud in sight and the promise of a pleasant day. That is a nice prospect awaiting us. What more could we ask?"

Lord Pace agreed with her and they set off in the direction indicated by Claudia in a congenial mood. Since Dorothy Cork knew the area quite as well as did Claudia, there was little need to offer details to her.

Elliot rode alongside Lady Dunston who flirted discreetly with him. He appeared to enjoy the exchange. But then, Lady Dunston was a very eligible widow who had no attachments and was extremely lovely. So far there hadn't as yet been a word of gossip about her and that would be of interest to Elliot.

Olivia Greene listened with flattering attention to whatever Lodge had to say. Hawke couldn't help but think that if she wanted to attract his interest, she couldn't find a better way to do so. Lodge might be quiet but he was a prodigious thinker, and to have someone willing to listen to those thoughts was more than a little agreeable to him. If his expression was anything to go by, the vicar might find the woman who had tried so hard to please him pleasing someone else instead.

The lane was a trifle dusty so that when the group ambled across the first of the fields it was a welcome change. Knowing this area as well as he did, Hawke suddenly realized that he might achieve his wishes in regard to Claudia. Or at least he might make a step in the right direction. There was a nice little path he recalled. Perhaps he might entice her to the view. Not that he intended to go beyond what was acceptable to the prim widow. He hoped to make her aware that she had missed a great deal with that nodcock of a husband she'd married.

The scenery was truly admirable. Claudia couldn't have chosen a route guaranteed to be more pleasant at this time of year. The foliage was arrayed in ripe, mellow hues; the winds normally found in spring were now soft, gentle. Indeed, it was an excellent setting for what he had in mind.

"Miss Cork is right," Claudia said suddenly, breaking into Hawke's musings. "The day could not be bettered. I trust you will enjoy the simple repast awaiting us."

He agreed that the weather was auspicious for the outing so hastily planned. That Claudia had roped in her friends and staff to arrange the day was all too likely. She had been reluctant to be alone with him with only Edward as company. Hawke suppressed a grin. Apparently the widow felt uneasy around him. Good.

He edged forward to instruct Edward on a few points of handling his pony. Jem Groom had done well in tutoring the lad in the basics. A gentle amble was precisely what was needed to give the boy confidence.

The route wandered across a narrow bridge, then over a few gentle hills and around an outcrop of rock. Hawke, dropping back to ride beside Claudia, found himself lured into complacency, a sense of detachment, if you will. His plan would succeed. All he needed to do was adhere to it and the widow would be his.

At last they rode over a rise and down into the meadow that was obviously their goal. He was pleased. Claudia had selected the precise site he had hoped she would. The viewing spot he recalled was but a stone's throw from here. He smiled.

From the number of baskets being arranged on quickly erected tables, it seemed there would be ample food for all.

Hawke wondered how Claudia and the others in her household had managed to whip together an alfresco meal for this size group, not to mention find Miss Cork. That the young woman could actually ride properly, was reasonably pretty, and as far as Hawke could see wasn't boring Pace to death was amazing.

"Miss Cork does well." He turned to Claudia in the hope she might explain the puzzle.

"Miss Cork is amenable to spontaneous parties. She is also a dear young woman. She has a sizable portion she will receive upon her marriage, as will Olivia, not to forget Miss Mary Alcock." Claudia glanced at Hawke and he observed a lurking amusement in her fine blue eyes.

"Portions are well and good; however, some things are more important—like character and poise." They approached the area where the servants arranged the picnic. "Mrs. Tibbins has obviously done you proud," he added to change the topic.

At the question in his voice, Claudia tilted her chin.

"Mrs. Tibbins prides herself on coping with anything that occurs, as does Cook. You will find sliced ham and various cheeses, a variety of rolls and salads, and I think she added a seed cake. I believe that is a favorite of yours, my lord. Cook is under the impression you are to be placated." Claudia's eyes held a glimmer of sauciness.

"What? Placated? For heaven's sake why?" Hawke considered the cook might want to please him, but placate?

"You are Edward's other guardian and as a man probably have more standing than a stepmother as far as the courts are concerned. I fancy that on any point of contention your wishes would be favored." She pursed her mouth into an adorably prim line. "We still have to decide on Eton for the coming year. Were you to insist, you would likely prevail." It was clear that Claudia was opposed to any such plan.

"Would that it were so," he muttered, thinking if that were the case, Edward would be off to Eton and the beautiful Claudia would be in his arms without any interruptions.

She tossed him a questioning look that he totally ignored. Nudging Kismet forward, he advised Edward on guiding his pony to where Jem Groom could assist him. The lad had done extremely well. He was a born rider and had required little prompting. Hawke got down from Kismet and looped the reins on a sturdy tree.

He helped Claudia dismount, wishing he might gather her in his arms instead of decorously setting her on her feet. He did allow her to brush against him. By the expression on her face, she was well aware of what he had done.

Jem led the pony away before returning to collect Claudia's mare, and prepared to secure it.

"Folly is indeed a gentle beast," Claudia said with a pat on the pretty chestnut mare as she was led away.

She watched as Jem expertly looped the reins around a tall birch.

"I thought you two would suit." Hawke suspected he smirked, for his judgement had once again been proven correct.

Dorothy Cork rode up to where Hawke stood at Claudia's side. "I am going to take Olivia and Mr. Lodge with us to see the view from the far side of the meadow. What time do you wish us to return?" She sat at ease on her mount, her brown hair curling nicely about a pretty face, her seat utterly perfect on her horse. Her deep blue habit turned her green eyes rather blueish and made her delicate porcelain complexion even more attractive. The more one looked at her, the better she became.

Claudia set a time, then turned to see Adela and Lord Elliot ambling along. They were deep in a discussion on something of obvious interest to them both. They dismounted and handed the reins to Jem Groom before joining Hawke and Claudia. Hawke gave his friend a significant look—one that was returned in full measure.

"Lady Dunston and I thought we might walk over to the stream to watch Edward." Elliot placed a hand beneath Lady Dunston's elbow. "And perhaps there is something else of interest to be seen?" He didn't ask for suggestions.

"Excellent," Hawke assured them while edging Claudia away in the opposite direction. To her he quietly added, "I should like to show you the view from this direction. Come?"

She made no objection, to his satisfaction. She looped her habit skirt over one arm, then strolled along at his side. "And may I ask what this particular view might be?"

"You will see soon enough." He guided her up the rather narrow path until they reached a rise, beyond which the path plunged almost straight down to the gentle valley below. In the distance Hawke's Rest could be seen, delineated clearly in the sharp light of the sun.

"How perfectly lovely," Claudia exclaimed with apparent delight.

Hawke thought her enthusiasm sounded real. He had not considered her a woman who would fake something so mundane as a reaction to the view of his estate. But he wanted her to see how extensive it was and also to take note that it looked to be in good heart.

"My steward and I take pride in the progress of the estate. This is a bird's-eye view of it. While you cannot see details, you can get an overview of what we have accomplished since my father died. He was more interested in London Society than in the land that gave him the wherewithal to enjoy that company."

He could see she was taken aback at his words. "I somehow never thought of you as someone who took interest in his crops, the farm—all that," she concluded vaguely. "You have always been described as a . . . a man involved in Society."

He wondered what she had been about to say before she paused. Did she label him a rake? A few did. He wasn't, of course. Not that he didn't socialize, but his activities were somewhat limited in scope. An opera dancer, perhaps, or a fetching and very available widow might capture his interest for a time. As a rule, he prided himself in being discriminating.

Placing his arm carefully about her shoulders, drawing her closer to his side, he waited to see her reaction. None came. Taking heart, he turned her so that she faced him. Her eyes held a touch of wariness in them, and there was a guarded expression on her face. "Lord Hawke?"

He didn't respond to her questioning. A darted glance told him they were utterly alone. Instead, he gathered her close to him and proceeded to correct the kiss that had gone so wrong the other day. This time he would not be so stupid as to charge her with kissing like a spinster.

Claudia had suspected Lord Hawke had an ulterior motive for the morning ride. She had done what she could to arrange that all would be circumspect. There wasn't a soul who could possibly object to the inclusion of so many in the picnic. *And if,* that little voice inside her head taunted, *you imagined Lord Hawke wanted to get you to himself, who is to know*?

He was undoubtedly a master at his art of seducing ladies. All thought of how he had acquired such skill swirled away in the depths of his onslaught as his arms wrapped around her, a band of tender steel. There was little she might do other than to submit . . . and enjoy. For enjoy the kiss, she did. She yielded to the temptation of his lips as he proceeded to give her a lesson in the expertise involved in such an activity. Undoubtedly he thought it was a lesson her husband had neglected, and he was certainly right at that.

In all her life she had never experienced anything remotely like this kiss. It took her a moment to realize the kiss had gone further than she—and possibly he—realized. The top buttons to her habit had been released. It was not until his kisses touched the side of her neck, lingered on tender skin, sent little thrills down her sensitive spine, that she realized what he had done. She scarce knew what to think, let alone say.

At last she was allowed to inch away from him. She knew she most likely wore a highly bemused expression. She simply could not summon indignant words, much less a slap to that handsome face. "I thought better of you, my lord," she said at long last, trying to sound at least a little incensed. She had the immense satisfaction of seeing he looked a trifle rattled himself.

"I had to correct what happened the other day. I was totally wrong, you see. I was hasty, and I picked the wrong time and place in which to kiss you. *This* is a step in the right direction." A rather wolfish grin curved his lips, and his eyes danced with something lurking in them. Triumph, perhaps?

"I do not think I shall inquire what that direction might be, my lord." Claudia clung to formality. If she didn't, she might well beg the rotten rake to kiss her again! Never in her life had she been so shaken or so stirred to the depths of her being. A part of her quite longed to beg him to resume his attentions. "I believe we had best return to the meadow where the others are. The picnic, you recall?"

Hawke was well pleased with his progress and nodded his agreement to her suggestion. He hadn't realized he had so much patience, although he had suspected he would require a certain amount of the trait. He sensed that his pursuit of the luscious widow would take longer than he had hoped. He thought he had time on his side, however. He could remain at Hawke's Rest as long as needed, and she had no place to go. He doubted she would leave as long as Edward was here. As soon as the lad went off to Eton, she would be free. And Hawke intended to act with dispatch to secure his aim, if not before, then after.

The widow would be his. That is, unless he perished of frustration before then.

They found the meadow filled with activity. Miss Cork and the others had returned from their excursion to join Elliot and Lady Dunston by the stream. Edward was excitedly holding up a small trout—enough to feed one person, perhaps.

"Mama, see what I caught."

Claudia saw, and smiled. The others appeared well pleased with their day. She hastily joined her stepson, offering praise and expressing her delight in his accomplishment. That she managed to shake off Lord Hawke's possessive hold on her arm at the same moment was her own small victory.

Naturally it didn't last very long. In short order she

found herself once again close to his side, indulging in the delicious foods that he selected for her. They sat on cushions brought from the Hall, Hawke seeing to it that Claudia was comfortable. He was most amiable. Well, perhaps he'd decided he had won whatever contest he'd devised.

The others chatted away with ease. Claudia tried to join in the casual conversation but found it difficult. Inwardly she still remained unsettled from that stirring kiss. What would it be like to have him kiss her as he so obviously wanted? She realized her buttons were still undone and bent forward while she did them up again, hoping that no one would pay her the slightest notice or guess how they came to that state.

"When will you paint Edward's dragon plate?" Hawke inquired. "I would like to see that when you are done." He leaned over to direct his remark to her, excluding the others. His smile beguiled and those intensely blue eyes seemed to see far more than they ought.

"It is difficult to paint with company in the house." She wasn't certain if she could even recall how she intended to represent the dragon. Edward had told her what he wanted. Trying to create that image was something else.

"Lady Dunston, you would have no objection to Claudia painting that plate for Edward, would you?" Hawke turned to the charming widow with that beguiling smile still on his face.

Claudia saw the look he gave Adela and knew the reply before it was given.

"Object? Of course not. As matter of fact, I would like to watch her paint. If she doesn't mind, that is." Adela turned to fix her gaze on Claudia as though attempting to assess her state of mind.

Claudia nodded her assurance. Speaking was a trifle difficult at the moment. Hawke was too close to her. He upset her equilibrium too easily. She was determined to remain aloof. And if that wasn't the silliest bit of nonsense that ever popped into her head she didn't know. How did a woman remain aloof from a man who seemed determined to lure her, not only into his arms but his bed as well? Not that she would go, mind you.

"I understand you intend to proceed with draining that piece of bottomland," Hawke said, sounding disapproving.

"I thought we decided that it was none of your affair, my lord. My bailiff agrees with me on the matter. I read an article on the subject and want to try it out on that bit of land." She glared at him as she edged away, sliding her cushion as she did.

Hawke thought a moment and shook his head. "Foolishness." He might want the widow and that strip of land along with her, but he wasn't about to fawn over her to the extent that he agreed with stupid proposals. This was a stupid proposal.

"I suppose you are among those who think a woman knows nothing of such matters as managing land." She took a savage bite from a chicken leg and Hawke had the feeling she would like to do some violence to him if she could think of a way without killing him.

"I did not say that, precisely. I merely question the productivity of such action. Will it pay for itself?" He lounged at her side, watching the fluctuating color on her lovely cheeks. "You actually think that land is worth the effort?"

"Draining it is not all that costly. I suppose you worry that the water will affect your property." She gave him a sidelong glance before attacking the chicken again.

"Now that you mention it . . ."

"Mr. Fry studied the situation quite thoroughly and is satisfied there will be no problem. My bailiff is a careful man." Claudia placed the bone on her plate, then proceeded to sip lemonade from her glass before trying a bit of ham.

"I trust you will change your mind when you see all that is involved in the scheme." He knew she hadn't thought of all the side effects. He knew there had to be several even if he couldn't think of them on the spur of the moment.

"Trust is relying on someone. I do not think I trust you on this, my lord. I doubt if you were reading treatises on crop management or the like while in London. Somehow being a leading light in Society doesn't seem compatible with that notion."

Hawke wished the others were not present. He wanted nothing more than to grab Claudia, shake some sense into her, then kiss her until she forgot all about the scheme for the bottomland. Her bailiff was likely under her thumb—a yes person.

"I suppose," she added with a touch of coyness, "that you disapprove of the plan to buy a hardy northern breed of sheep to improve our local stock? Mr. Fry thinks my proposal quite sensible." Her glance was positively flirtatious.

"Hmpf." Hawke repressed the strong desire to tell Claudia she needed a new bailiff, one that wasn't an easy prey for a beautiful face with an absurd idea. "Utter nonsense."

She gave him an offended look that stabbed him to the quick. What on earth possessed him to quibble with her on points over which he had no control?

Rising from her cushion, she walked over to speak quietly with Edward. She then settled on the grass at his side while she inspected his plate, suggesting he have some cheese with his bun. Her oblique glance at Hawke was cool.

Hawke studied her down-bent head, wondering how he managed to place himself in a position where she no longer trusted him. If she ever had, that is. As of this moment, they were in a cautious neutrality, although Claudia looked as though she would gladly set off for Fairfax Hall without him. He would have to discuss the matter of the bottomland drainage with his steward. He was willing to admit he might be wrong, but only after conferring with his own steward, a man he felt superior to the all-knowing Mr. Fry in all respects. Logan might be an older man, but he was awake on all suits as evidenced by his management of Hawke's Rest. The tenants had prospered, as had the estate in general.

As to the sheep, he allowed as though she might have something in her plan. Logan would have a few words to offer on that matter as well.

When the picnic drew to an end, the assorted riders mounted and rode back toward the Hall. Claudia remained for a few minutes, giving directions to her staff before Jem Groom lifted Edward to his saddle, then assisted her to Folly's saddle. She gave Hawke a distant nod and rode off with Edward at her side.

Hawke found himself quite cut out. He shook his head. How was he to reestablish himself in Claudia's good graces now? For a man noted for his polished address, he found that nothing he did appeared to work well with the comely widow.

Chapter Nine

*T*wo somewhat tired and dusty ladies entered the sitting room, each one intent upon finding a comfortable place to rest.

Mrs. Tibbins followed them, tsking and tutting all the way. "I gather you had a fine day. Master Edward is in a fine state, he is. Happy as a lark, he is. Tea . . ." she mumbled as she left the sitting room for the kitchen.

Adela sank onto a high-backed armchair while Claudia settled for the sofa. She placed her feet up, wishing to rest, for it had been such a long time since she had last ridden. The peace and quiet of the sitting room was precisely what she needed. She would ache from head to toe come tomorrow.

"I shall rest my bones a while before attempting to go up to my room," Claudia said, ignoring her trailing habit. It was dusty and she should be more careful of the sofa. Widows tended to think of things like the cost of replacement and so forth.

"You will feel better after a hot soak in a bath. I suspect I will as well." Adela thought for a few moments before adding, "You seemed at variance with Lord Hawke on the way home. I trust it is nothing that time will not cure?"

"That is impossible to say. The man personifies aggravation. I am not certain how best to deal with him." The war on her nerves had worn her to a frazzle. Sparring with Lord Hawke made her pulse race and her nerves taut. She sensed he knew how he affected her. She wasn't always totally coherent when she replied to one of his many questions or remarks. She wasn't even sure what she said to all he had asked. After his kiss she was a mere pool of sensation.

As to sparring with him regarding Eton, or the bottomland, or the sheep improvement, she couldn't even recall what she had said—if he had asked her a question about them, or argued with her. He did not approve of what she proposed for the bottomland, she recalled. As to Eton? She would consider the matter. The sheep purchase was none of his affair. Most likely he would be in London when they arrived come spring.

She was aware of Adela's speculative gaze, but reluctant to put her feelings into words . . . if such a thing was possible. How did you describe the confusion that left you breathless?

"I believe that all went well," Adela said. "Everyone appeared to enjoy the day. Dorothy Cork was certainly a nice addition to the party. She is a delightful girl and appeared to get along well with Lord Pace." Adela removed her charming hat and set it on a small table. "However, *you* do not seem very pleased, my dear Claudia." She gave Claudia a curious look.

Still uncertain just how much she wished to reveal to her good friend, Claudia hesitated. She studied the pattern of the carpet for a few moments and twiddled her thumbs while she considered the matter.

"Ah, something did happen. I suspected Lord Hawke had somehow overstepped himself considering the icy silence pervading the trip home." There was a question in Adela's voice, yet she did not probe for an answer.

"Lord Hawke is so sure he knows everything there

is to know about farming!" Claudia said with exasperation, avoiding the matter of the kiss. "As though a London gentleman would read up on such a topic. *He* thinks I ought not drain the bottomland! Of all the nerve! What a pity it is that he also happens to be Edward's guardian. I cannot forbid him to come here for any reason." Her sigh was heartfelt.

"How odd. I had the feeling that the two of you found one or two points upon which to agree. I shan't ask you what happened on your little walk . . . but you did not appear ready to do battle when you rejoined us." Adela took her hat to fan herself, looking warm, yet utterly charming.

"We were able to see his estate from the viewpoint," Claudia murmured, feeling slightly guilty regarding her enjoyment of that stolen kiss. She suspected that a faint rosiness had crept into her cheeks. She felt warm.

"I see. And the view caused a blush? Oh, my dear!" Adela chuckled.

They heard the sound of footsteps in the hall and ceased talking as Olivia and Dorothy entered the sitting room.

"What a splendid day," Olivia cried with enthusiasm. "I had no notion that Mr. Lodge was such a fount of information. And so interesting too." She plumped down on the chair near the fireplace, beaming a smile at the others. "He is not the least prosy. He offers all matter of knowledge in an entertaining manner. I truly enjoyed his company."

Dorothy gave Claudia a demure smile. "Thank you so very much for asking me to join you all. Lord Pace proved to be a most congenial companion. As Olivia said, it was a splendid day." She paused, seeming uncertain whether she ought to sit, which she did when Claudia waved her to a chair. "Forgive me for not rising. My ankle, you see," she concluded vaguely, although her ankle truly didn't trouble her any longer.

She was simply exhausted from dealing with Lord Hawke.

"And Edward caught a fish in addition to riding his pony." Olivia gave Claudia a confused look. "I was under the impression that just you and Lord Hawke were to accompany Edward on his first ride of any distance."

"I thought it prudent to enlarge the party. I'd not wish the vicar or Mrs. Alcock to find fault with my conduct." Claudia hoped her expression was as bland as her words.

"Oh, to be sure," Olivia replied, frowning over her thoughts. "He is all that is proper, as is Mrs. Alcock."

It was as though her words had conjured up the vicar, Claudia wryly admitted as she heard his familiar voice speaking to Mrs. Tibbins in the entryway.

"Well, what have we here? I stopped by earlier only to find that Edward—and you—had gone out for a ride with Lord Hawke. I trust the lad enjoyed his pony?" He ignored everyone but Claudia, quite as though she was alone in the room.

Claudia hated the note of censure in his tone. It was none of his dratted business if she went out riding with her stepson. Or with Lord Hawke, for that matter.

Olivia leaped into the breach. "We had an impromptu picnic today. There were eight of us, plus Edward, of course. It was most charming." She lifted her chin slightly. "I found it quite instructive, Mr. Lodge being such a fount of wisdom."

"And Lord Pace was so very kind," Dorothy Cork said in her quiet voice. She darted a glance at Olivia before turning her attention to her hands, now neatly folded in her lap.

"Lord Elliot is very amiable in his ways as well." Adela spoke up, adding her piece. "Lord Hawke's friends are all that is agreeable. Lady Fairfax offered us a delicious collation and a pleasant ride in the country. I must say, you have some very pretty scenery about here. I shouldn't wonder if Lord Hawke's guests stay with him for a time. Titled, handsome gentlemen who are also wealthy are always welcome. Have you not seen it to be so, vicar?" She offered him a sly smile.

The vicar was gasping like a landed trout. Fortunately Mrs. Tibbins entered at that moment with a tray holding all that was necessary for a late afternoon tea. "Here's just the thing for you all, for I know you must be perishing for a cup of tea."

"Do sit down, Vicar Woodley, and join us for tea." The moment he had appeared Claudia had discreetly lowered her feet to the floor and edged to one end of the sofa. Now she gestured to the far end, hoping he would not attempt to sit close to her. She *would* have to be the one sitting on the sofa!

"Miss Greene, Lady Dunston, and Miss Cork went along?" he finally said, looking somewhat dazed. What had he thought? That she had ridden off with only Lord Hawke for company along with Edward? Evidently he had not asked, merely assumed, as he was wont to do.

"Well, with those friends of Lord Hawke's visiting, we thought it would be kind to include them in a ride—to show off our lovely countryside, you know." Claudia tended to the tea, pouring out for the women, then the vicar. Lastly, she took refuge in her own cup of the steaming brew.

Mrs. Tibbins, knowing how much the vicar enjoyed her scones, had included a plate of them on the tray. Claudia offered him the plate and he absently took it, setting the plate beside him on the Pembroke table instead of offering it to the ladies as would have been proper. "I find this all very disturbing." Disturbed, he might be, it did not prevent him from making immediate inroads on the scones.

"Why?" Adela inquired. "With such a large group

we were all well chaperoned. What could possibly happen on an innocent ride in the country?" She took a sip of tea, then added, "Scenery is always a beneficial study, is it not?"

Claudia was thankful she wasn't required to say a word.

"Edward . . . and those men from London?" the vicar muttered.

"They were most kind to the lad," Olivia assured him. She gave her heretofore hero an assessing look. Since Olivia loved scones but was too polite to ask him to share them, she doubtless felt a touch peevish. The vicar was being quite selfish, did he but realize it.

Miss Cork added, "Lord Fairfax even caught a small trout. And I believe he did smashingly well on his pony. Did not Lord Hawke say he rode as though born to the saddle?" She looked to the others to confirm her recollection.

"That he did," Claudia managed to reply. The expression on Olivia's face was priceless. What a pity that the vicar was too absorbed with the image of Lord Hawke and Claudia on a riding party or he would have seen Olivia's disillusionment.

"I see." What the vicar thought he saw was not revealed. He did not look pleased, however.

"So," Adela concluded, "you see before you a quartet of very tired but happy ladies who have had a stimulating day exploring nature. Surely you approve of our enjoying God's creation, vicar?" She assumed a virtuous expression.

"Oh, indeed, indeed," Vicar Woodley replied uncertainly. He gave Claudia an aggrieved look. "I suppose it is only to be expected, Lord Hawke being Edward's guardian and all."

"How true," Adela said smoothly. "Lord Hawke is most concerned with the education of his ward."

"We do have many things to discuss. You realize

that his lordship insists I must send Edward off to Eton this fall." Debating with herself for a few moments, Claudia added, "Do you think he is sufficiently prepared for such a change?"

"Prepared? Well, I have taught him for some months now. I should think he is tolerably ready to join other boys his age. Of course, if you have qualms about sending him away, I could continue to tutor him a bit longer."

He gave Claudia such a fawning smile she longed to toss a pillow—or a statue or anything else handy—at the man. She hoped that Olivia was seeing him with opened eyes. Her afternoon with a gentleman who was equally educated and most polite, and who treated her as any lady could wish to be treated, should help. Let the vicar turn to Mary Alcock, for pity's sake.

Olivia rose from her chair, placed her cup and saucer carefully on the tray, then announced, "Excuse me. I believe I shall retire to my room." Without a glance at the vicar she marched from the sitting room, like a galleon at full sail.

Claudia exchanged a look with Adela, trying very hard not to laugh. She didn't know what was more amusing, Olivia turning her nose up at the vicar or the vicar looking aghast at her ignoring him. After all, he had been accustomed to her obsequious attentions for some time now.

At last the man left, but not until he had demolished the pile of scones and two cups of tea.

"We all need a rest. Dorothy, why do you not stay here?"

"Thank you kindly, but my mother expects me." She curtsied nicely to Adela before preparing to leave.

"Well, I expect those gentlemen will seek our company again. Ask your mother if you might remain here for a few days. It is so pleasant to have company and I daresay Lord Pace would welcome the sight of you again. I will send a note with you now." Claudia rose, found paper and pen in her small desk, and immediately wrote a persuasive missive to Dorothy's mother.

After her agreement and blushing departure, Adela and Claudia retired to their rooms. Claudia hoped she could soon see the last of the vicar. As to what she hoped in regard to Lord Hawke, she didn't know.

The men straggled into the solidly built brick home of Georgian design. Although a mere sixty years old, it had the look of a well-loved home, well cared for as well. By common consent they headed for the library, a restful room with book-lined walls, excellent lighting from many windows, and more importantly, comfortable chairs. The amber tinted walls had several fine paintings hung on them, and the books were an interesting combination of old and recent printings. The richly hued carpet muffled their steps.

"You ought to be pleased," Elliot said to his good friend Hawke. "It was a day well spent. I must admit I saw a side to Lady Dunston I'd not seen before. She is a most attractive lady." He'd followed Hawke into the library, then poured a glass of canary before finding a large armchair in which to lounge.

Hawke nodded, sinking back into the comfortable leather chair by the fireplace. "You knew her in London, I gather."

"Lodge, what say you of the day?" Elliot inquired of the more quiet gentleman of the group.

"I found Miss Greene to be uncommonly sensible. She is rather pretty as well." He raised his glass of sherry in a mock toast to the absent plumpish lady.

"Not to mention her sizable portion. Claudia informed me that the Cork girl and Miss Greene are both well dowered." Hawke roused himself to impart this information. If these three were actually in search of wives, this was helpful intelligence. While they had money enough, more was always welcome.

Lord Pace leaned back in his chair, sipping the sherry he had poured for himself. "I must add that Miss Cork is a charming girl. Amiable, too. Doesn't talk your head off. Dashed good seat." He stretched out his legs before him, looking to see if his boots had been scratched when they walked to see the view.

"Considering that you spend a large part of your time on horseback, that is high praise, indeed." Hawke grinned at his horse-mad friend.

Elliot turned to Hawke. "And you? How did you fare with your coguardian today? It seemed rather chilly on the way home. She looked somewhat annoyed when you returned from viewing your estate. Did you have a disagreement?"

Hawke shrugged. "A small matter came up. I want to discuss it with Ben Logan first before I say anything more to her on the subject. She raised a puzzling issue." It was all he was going to say on the question for the present. If Ben thought draining the bottomland a plausible plan Hawke didn't want to appear an idiot. However, he couldn't help but wonder what effect the draining would have on his property.

They sat for a time, discussing the day, what else was to be seen in the area, and the prospect of dinner as well as what they might do the next day.

Before long the three guests went up to their assigned rooms, leaving Hawke on his own. Rather than go up, he went directly to the small estate office in the back of the house. As expected he found his steward there busy at some paperwork.

"Logan, are you familiar with the bottomland on the Fairfax property?" Hawke paused just inside the door, wondering how much to reveal.

"Of course. You pass it when you leave by the south road. Why?" Logan pushed back his chair to study his employer. Keen gray eyes studied Hawke from under grizzled brows. He had served the Hawke family for many years and if anyone knew the land, it was Logan.

"Lady Fairfax says she plans to drain it. Do you think that wise? Would it impact my land?" Hawke crossed to the desk where a stack of papers awaited his perusal.

"I think her bailiff would make certain that your property would not be adversely affected. I believe there is a way to channel the water so it actually might prove to be beneficial to you." Logan drew forth a few papers that obviously wanted Hawke's signature. He would sign them before leaving the office after he got a few more answers.

Hawke twisted his mouth in a wry grimace. Not only would it not harm his land, it might actually be of benefit. Good grief.

"But would it actually be that positive a thing for her to do? Truly beneficial, considering the cost of drainage?" There had to be a flaw in her plan. True, she administered Edward's estate. But as his other guardian, shouldn't he approve of any drastic changes?

"That is something her ladyship will have to decide. From what Fry tells me, she reads everything she can find on farming and land management." Logan allowed a partial smile to cross his lips, likely knowing how Hawke might feel about the proposal.

"That figures. I might have known she is a bluestocking," Hawke muttered. "Thank you for the information. I spoke with her on the subject earlier, but had no idea what impact such a plan would have on my land." He thought that was sufficient explanation. At least, it was all he was prepared to offer.

Logan nodded, turning his attention back to the stack of papers on the desk before him. "Would you sign these letters, sir?"

Hawke studied the first paper, then signed, doing the same with the others. He left the office feeling disgruntled. Why, he wasn't sure. He did not like being bested by a mere female, for one thing.

A steaming bath awaited him in his room. He

stripped off his garments, then sank into the depths of his tub. He would have to apologize, he supposed. Staring at the ceiling, he wondered what would happen next. Would she accept his apology in a civilized manner? He supposed she would. She was a lady to her fingertips—even when confronted with an overbearing male.

Dinner was quiet that evening as Edward remained in the nursery with his nanny, leaving three pensive women.

"Delicious mushroom soup, Claudia. I must get Cook's recipe. Mine doesn't do nearly as well." Adela placed her spoon in her soup dish before blotting her mouth with the pristine white square of linen.

Claudia attempted to enter into the conversation with some sort of enthusiasm and thought she did well enough.

Olivia had little to say. Claudia wondered if she was still mulling over the foolish way the vicar had behaved while here earlier. She, for one, would not be sorry if he ceased to present himself, ostensibly to tutor Edward. Then she chastised herself for her thoughts. Of course he tutored the lad. Merely because she had taken him into dislike was no reason to cast aspersions on his ability.

They left the table, wandering into the sitting room. Adela played a bit on the pianoforte. Olivia dug out some knitting. It looked like a scarf for Edward. Could that yarn be Eton blue? Claudia wasn't positive, but thought it might be. So Olivia was sure that Lord Hawke would win out in the dispute, was she?

Ignoring her guests for a few minutes, Claudia considered the matter. She had heard things about Dr. Keate, the head master of the school, that did not please her. Supposedly he was given to flogging students for any infraction. Edward was not a naughty child, but just how demanding was Dr. Keate?

"Adela," she said at last, "what do you know of Dr. Keate at Eton?"

"I understand he is a gifted scholar, but a severe disciplinarian. You worry about Edward?" Adela left the pianoforte to join Claudia and Olivia near the small fire that took the chill from the room.

"I am. He isn't truly a sensitive boy, but I cannot help wonder if it is a sensible thing to do as Lord Hawke insists."

"Think on it a while. Nothing is gained by rushing," Olivia counseled. "Surely Eton can wait for a bit?"

Claudia nodded her agreement, content to let it slide, to allow things to take care of themselves. She stared broodingly at the Eton blue yarn in Olivia's lap.

Chapter Ten

*H*e would have to apologize. Quite how to best accomplish the deed without making an utter ass of himself or seeming too eager to ingratiate himself with the widow he wasn't certain. Perhaps he would talk to her bailiff first just to ascertain the chap had actually studied the matter of the bottomland and knew what he was talking about. No point in doing penance unless it was necessary.

Pace and Lodge consumed a hearty breakfast while he and Elliot lingered over their coffee, having polished off their meal earlier. Hawke stared into his cup, trying to decide the most effective approach.

"What did you learn about the problem that reared its head?" Elliot said quietly, casting a speculative look at Hawke.

"Logan said it was not a bad idea for her to drain her bottomland. Not only that, but it might actually benefit my property," Hawke concluded dryly.

"Draining bottomland?" Pace queried. "I read something on that not long ago. So your pretty neighbor plots to drain a bit of land?" Pace helped himself to another scone and strawberry preserves, sharing the pot with Lodge.

"Plot being the significant word there." Hawke grimaced, wondering what else lurked in the lovely widow's mind.

"Didn't you once tell me that there is a strip of land now part of that estate that once was yours?" Elliot idly crumbled the remainder of his scone while he watched Hawke.

"Right." Hawke took a deep breath. "My grandfather lost it in a game of cards to little Edward's great-grandfather. It now is in the possession of Lady Fairfax, given to her as part of her jointure." Hawke stared at his empty cup as though it might provide advice.

"Would she sell?" Elliot wondered. "I mean, what would or could she possibly do with the land?" He sipped his cooling coffee while watching Hawke. Pace and Lodge also watched but didn't join in the discussion, intent upon finishing their meal.

Hawke grinned. Not wishing his friends to know the depth of his interest in the delicious Lady Fairfax he joked, "Well, I could marry the lady and it would save me the price."

Elliot frowned. "She seems rather nice."

"Indeed, she is," Hawke agreed with alacrity.

Slade entered the breakfast room. As usual, the butler's manner was firmly in place. "Master Edward is here, my lord. He rode his pony over, I believe in the understanding you would wish to see him?" Slade still referred to the young Lord Fairfax by his previous style.

"Show him in here, please." To Elliot he added, "I am not quite ready to take on his instruction at this hour."

The lad shyly entered the room, gazing with respect at the four *tonnish* gentlemen at the table. His eyes were wide with admiration. Obviously these gentlemen were far and away above the vicar. Two now perused newspapers, the others obviously chatted. He focused on Lord Hawke.

"I am doing ever so much better today. Humbug is a very good sort of pony and I am ever so thankful you found him for me." He sidled up to where Hawke sat at the far end of the oval table. "You ought to see me ride."

"Well, I am glad you like him so well. Did you wish to ask me something in particular?"

"No." He paused, plainly having something on his mind but hesitant to proceed. "Mama is having a stone wall built for me. It will have a channel, she said, so I can sail my boats without getting all dirty. Were you allowed to get dirty when you were a boy?" He stood, hands behind him, respectful but curious.

Hawke grinned at his friends, then returned his gaze to Edward. "I should say we all contrived to get rather grubby as lads. Your mama no doubt thinks this channel will be interesting for you."

"She said I have worn out too many breeches. I s'pose it makes extra washing." Edward wrinkled his forehead as though attempting to think of other reasons he had to stay clean. "I rather think I like the stream better. There won't be any fishes in the stone channel, will there? And it is very close to the terrace. Mama can watch me while I play." The last words were uttered with resignation.

"Look at it this way: you will have a jolly time sailing your boats on the water without worrying about a scold."

"Clever idea," Lodge offered from behind his paper.

Edward did not look the slightest convinced.

"Tell you what, I will come out now and watch you ride. That is what you want, isn't it?" Hawke inquired.

"If you please, sir. Humbug is a dandy pony and I think I could teach him a trick or two. If I knew how. I would like to very much. Do you think you could show me how to teach him a trick? Sir?" Edward fastened wide brown eyes on his friend. Tousled curls tumbled down on his brow, his slim person stiff with hope.

Hawke exchanged a rueful look with Elliot, glancing at Pace and Lodge, who both seemed highly amused about something. "Yes, we will all join you in the stable yard. Lord Pace is something of an expert with training horses. I'll wager he has a trick up his sleeve."

The boy grinned before dashing off to his pony.

"I say, now, Hawke, that isn't fair. I might train a horse but hardly to do tricks," Pace scolded mildly.

"I need a witness or three if I am to proceed with this nonsense. Poor lad, no father and no one but that blasted vicar to look to for male advice." Hawke shared a grimace with Elliot. Both gentlemen had voiced strong opinions on the redheaded vicar. Young ladies might sigh over him, but he couldn't hold a candle to the gentlemen visiting. Olivia Greene had her eyes opened yesterday, unless he missed his guess. Lodge was far superior to the conceited vicar.

The four men left the breakfast room, wandering out to see how young Edward fared with his pony.

"The lad does well enough," Pace pronounced after a time of putting Humbug through his paces, Edward sitting as straight as humanly possible for a little boy.

They were in the process of devising a clever trick when it happened. A dog from one of the tenant farms came lolloping into the stable yard, barking and dashing around the pony, no doubt looking for Edward to play with him.

The problem was with the pony, which took great exception to this upstart dog that had no manners at all. The pony shied, jumping nervously, finally rearing up in a way that startled them all, including the pony. Quite terrified, the pony shook off his rider and Edward took a nasty tumble.

"That tears it," Hawke muttered as he ran to the boy's side. "Claudia will have my guts for garters if this lad is seriously injured."

Edward bravely bit his lip against pain, ignoring the few tears that squeezed out from behind tightly shut lids. "I think there is something the matter with my arm. It hurts dreadfully," he managed at last.

Hawke looked up to Elliot. "Send one of the grooms for Beemish. He's the local apothecary. The village doesn't warrant anything so grand as a doctor much less a surgeon."

Edward's eyes flashed open, tears vanished as he listened. "My arm won't have to be cut off, will it?"

"You will be right as rain in no time. I feel sure your mama would want to have that arm looked at, however. I'd not care to displease her. Be a brave lad while I carry you up to a bedroom."

Edward obeyed, wincing as they rounded the corner into the bedroom. He looked about him with mild curiosity at the grand room and the impressive bed hangings. It was a far cry from his nursery. Obviously this room was for grown-ups!

Slade entered to offer his services.

"Send a footman to Fairfax Hall to let her ladyship know her stepson has been injured. Invite her to come as soon as she pleases. And tell Mrs. Logan I want her up here immediately."

"Very good, sir." Slade bowed and left the room.

Hawke turned to Elliot. "I don't know how he does it but he manages to hurry without seeming to at all."

"My mama will be angry with me," Edward said, his face crumpling with worry. A tear-streaked, pale face made it unlikely he would get a scold.

"Your dear mama worries about you. Mamas tend to do things like that, you know." Hawke thought back to his childhood. Only his nanny had ever seen to any of his scrapes and injuries. He saw his parents on rare occasions when he was scrubbed and dressed in his best. They made it plain that while they liked him, the less they saw of him, the better. Hawke was glad that Claudia took interest in the lad. Although it did seem to him that she rather overdid her concern a trifle.

Over at Fairfax Hall Claudia wondered where Edward had got to. The boy had a talent for disappearing, slipping away from his nanny with ease. Claudia glanced up at the sound of footsteps. They were quick, and coming up to the front door.

Mrs. Tibbins hurried into the sitting room, her usually placid face screwed up with worry. "A footman from Hawke's Rest is here, ma'am. Wants to speak with you at once, urgent-like."

Puzzled, Claudia set aside her drawing of Edward's dragon to hasten to the front door. The footman awaited her in the Hawke gig. His face was troubled.

"Lady Fairfax, Lord Hawke said to fetch you. Lord Fairfax took a tumble from his pony and . . ." His sentence remained unfinished. Claudia cried out in alarm, then dashed back to get a bonnet and gloves, calling to Olivia to warn her something had happened to Edward.

"But what, dear Claudia? Do you wish to take something with you? The medicine chest? Anything?"

"They are sure to have all that is needed at Lord Hawke's house. I shall request Beemish be summoned." Claudia dashed out to the waiting gig, not caring what image she presented.

Olivia stood in the entry, a picture of concern while Claudia scrambled up in the gig, settling herself in a rush.

"What can you tell me of the accident?" she demanded of the young footman.

"Can't rightly say, my lady. I was in the house. First thing I knew was when Slade ordered me to fetch you. Lord Hawke seemed to think you'd want to be with your son at once."

With that Claudia had to be content for the moment.

In short order the footman drew the gig up before Hawke's house. The little carriage had barely ceased moving and Claudia was down from the seat, fairly running to the front door.

Slade had been watching for her. The door opened swiftly, with Slade unbending some from his usual austere manner. "I will take you to your son, my lady. Follow me."

Claudia scarce had time to glance about her in the rush up the stairs. Within seconds she was shown into a large bedroom with a vast bed at one end. Edward lay stretched out, his head on a large linen-covered pillow. His face was nearly as white as the linen. The four men stood around the bed, looking anxious.

"I'm sorry, Mama. I didn't mean to get hurt."

Ignoring the men, Claudia cautiously edged herself onto the bed, studying the boy to see where the injury might be. "I doubt anyone ever plans to get injured, love. Unfortunately, accidents do happen. Where does it hurt the most, dearest?"

"His arm seems to be the most tender," Lord Hawke inserted, placing a calming hand on Edward's shoulder.

"You have sent for Beemish?" she asked, her face etched with worry.

"Boys have taken tumbles for lo these many years, Lady Fairfax," Mr. Lodge said quietly. "I doubt he is seriously harmed. Be up and about in no time at all, I feel sure."

Claudia flashed him a dubious look, then began to peel off Edward's jacket, taking note that his left arm indeed had been hurt. Before she could remove his shirt, the apothecary entered.

"Thank heavens you are here. Edward fell from his pony and his left arm appears injured." She looked on in dismay as the apothecary cut the shirt open, then allowed her to slip the sleeve from his arm.

The elderly apothecary was skilled at soothing worried mothers. In no time at all he had sent the men away and put Claudia to holding the lad still. He examined the awkwardly held arm.

"His elbow is fractured," he muttered. He explained to Claudia the new method of setting bones he'd read about. She looked askance but accepted that Beemish knew best. He sent the maid down to the kitchen with his requests.

Mrs. Logan brought up a bowl of stiffly beaten egg whites and a roll of bandages. Claudia heroically remained to soothe Edward. Beemish quietly went about setting the arm, using the egg-white bandages he had read about and found most beneficial. Within a short time, the boy's arm was encased in a bandage—stiff, white, and resembling plaster. Edward was fascinated with the entire procedure once the pain of setting was over.

When Claudia went down to inquire about the possibility of a nightshirt, she found Olivia there with the needed item in hand.

"I knew there would be a few things required." Olivia looked her usual calm self, unlike Claudia's frazzled person.

"Olivia, what would I do without you!" Claudia repressed a strong desire to burst into tears.

Hawke appeared with Mrs. Logan at his side. Claudia handed the small nightshirt to the housekeeper. "Perhaps you might take this up? And see if there is anything else Mr. Beemish needs? I will return in a few minutes."

She turned to her son's unexpected host. "Thank you for sending for me so promptly. That boy is a genius at escaping from his nanny. Tell me how he came to fall."

Hawke guided her into the library. Olivia, Mr. Lodge, Lord Pace, and Lord Elliot followed. The aroma of leather-bound books, the faint hint of fine tobacco, and lavender-scented beeswax polish lingered in the air.

Claudia allowed herself to be guided to a fine leather chair, accepted a small glass of sherry, then awaited his account of the accident.

"He was riding Humbug and doing very well, mind you," Hawke explained. "A mutt from one of the tenant farms came up, intent upon playing with Edward, I suppose. At any rate, the pony took great exception to the dog and Edward ended up on the ground. It wasn't a great distance, but the way he fell, well—you know what happened to his arm. I can't begin to tell you how sorry I am this happened."

"Nothing in the world we might have done to prevent it," Mr. Lodge added from beside Olivia.

"That is true, Lady Fairfax," Lord Elliot agreed. "It simply happened in a flash."

"Trying to teach the pony a trick," Lord Pace inserted. "I haven't tried that before, but I must say that Edward and his pony were doing very well before that dog appeared on the scene." He helped himself to a glass of sherry, standing to one side while studying Claudia.

"I gather it was simply one of those stupid things that occur when you least expect them," Claudia murmured. She swallowed the last of her sherry, then rose from the chair. "Thank you all for your consideration of Edward—and of me. I believe I shall return to his side. Mr. Beemish must be about ready to leave by now. I would have remained, but I needed to know what had happened. He certainly did not require my help."

"Of course, dear Claudia. No one could be more concerned about little Edward than you are," Olivia exclaimed.

Claudia gave her friend and the others a dry smile, then left the library. Hawke followed her up the stairs.

"He is welcome to remain here until Beemish says he can be moved." He slipped his hand under her elbow, offering support.

Claudia paused at the top of the stairs, placing a hand over her heart. "How kind of you. I fear it will be dreadfully upsetting to your household. I doubt you are in the habit of catering to small boys who are abed after a fall."

"Nonsense," he said, smiling down into her eyes.

She experienced that fluttering sensation again that came over her whenever he got too close. How in the world would she be able to remain in this house with Lord Hawke while feeling as she did? His very touch sent strange tremors through her.

"Ah, I had a conversation with Logan and he seemed to think that draining that bottomland was not such a bad idea."

"Oh, Logan—your steward, I believe? Well, I am relieved you are not about to give me a scolding for being so terribly foolhardy. I imagine you wondered if it would adversely affect your property. It should not, as far as Fry could tell."

"So Logan seems to think." Hawke continued to stare at her, a most disconcerting sensation.

Claudia noted that Lord Hawke seemed rather ill at ease, with a dull flush on his cheeks.

"It seems I must beg your pardon. I felt that it was a rash, ill-conceived notion." His expression was such that she decided he thought she would turn shrewish at his explanation.

They paused outside Edward's bedroom. Claudia tamped down the annoyance that simmered at his assessment of her plan. It was to be expected. How was he to know that she and Fry had studied the matter at some length, the bailiff finally agreeing with her that it would add usable acreage to the estate.

"I suppose that is only to be expected, all things considered." She attempted to compose her nerves that were on edge. It wasn't surprising, given all that had happened.

"I gather your reading material extends beyond the

marble-boarded novels from Minerva Press." He leaned against the door surround, his intense gaze focused on her to her unease.

"I find the enrichment of the estate to be of worth, even if it means plowing through agricultural journals. Not that novels fail to entertain me. I greatly enjoy a book such as *Emma*." She waited to see what his reaction might be to this.

She wasn't to know, for the door opened and Mr. Beemish stood before them, his black bag in hand.

"Mr. Beemish! How does Edward do?" Lord Hawke stepped back, then walked with the apothecary to the top of the stairs.

"He had best remain here overnight. By tomorrow he ought to be able to withstand the short trip home. Fortunate he lives so close by. Keep the lad as quiet as you can; light food and sleep will not go amiss. I need not remind you to keep that arm dry. The egg-white bandage holds up well—normally. I see no reason why the lad should be kept in bed after today. Fretting is not good for lads. He will be less testy if he has something to amuse him. No riding his pony for some time, though." Mr. Beemish chuckled as though he was a great wit.

Claudia was aghast at such a cavalier attitude toward something as serious as a broken bone. "What about swelling? Will that bandage accommodate swelling should it occur?"

"I'll be over come tomorrow and have a look at him. Have Mrs. Tibbins collect all the eggs she can come morning. If I need to change the bandage, I'll need 'em."

Claudia had heard enough. She returned to Edward's side leaving Lord Hawke to escort the apothecary from the house. Closing the door behind her, she crossed to the vast bed. The boy was nearly lost in its great size. He seemed very frail and small to her worried eyes.

"I was very brave, Mama," Edward declared with obvious satisfaction. "Mr. Beemish said he never saw a boy as brave as I am. It hurt when he set my arm. I didn't cry a bit."

Claudia sat down on the bed. "I feel sure you are the very best, dearest. Lord Hawke will permit us to remain here until tomorrow when Mr. Beemish said you may go home." She said nothing about her doubts as to the wisdom of moving a boy with a broken arm so soon.

"Good. I shall have my toys, but Humbug will miss me." Edward gave a wistful look at the window.

"True. But if you obey Mr. Beemish you will be able to see Humbug soon. Likely the pony will know you are not quite up to snuff and unable to ride him."

With that, the boy closed his eyes and drifted off to sleep. She sat there quietly, wishing there was something she might do for the lad. Olivia scratched on the door and at Claudia's whispered command, entered.

"Oh my!" she exclaimed when she beheld the grandeur of the room. "How very nice. How long will Edward need to stay here? Should I bring you night-wear and other clothes?"

"Nightwear, only. I shall take Edward home on the morrow."

At Olivia's shocked expression, Claudia did her best to explain the apothecary's reasoning.

"Well, of course Beemish knows what is best," Olivia concluded, but in a decidedly doubtful voice.

One by one the others came to check on the boy. Claudia gave the men high marks for their concern. Her mind boggled at the thought of her late husband having that much care. She had an immensely improved feeling toward Lodge, Pace, and Elliot, considering them to be superior gentlemen.

Wouldn't it be lovely if Olivia turned her heart in the direction of the worthy Mr. Lodge? Eventually she would be a countess! Not that the fact would influence Olivia. She would give her heart to a man who was admirable.

Olivia left to fetch Claudia's nightwear and fresh underclothes for the morrow. The clock on the mantel ticked quietly away, the minutes dragging by on silent feet.

She had about dozed off when the door opened and Hawke entered the room.

"Time for dinner. A maid will sit with Edward while you join us below. Miss Greene has returned with Lady Dunston. She expressed concern for Edward and you as well. I gather she wonders at propriety with you in a bachelor household."

"Nothing could possibly happen, could it?" Claudia shot him a challenging look.

"You have placed me on my best behavior." He gave her the grin she found so irresistible and her insides fluttered far more than she liked. "There is a dressing room through that narrow door on the far side of the room. If you like, you may sleep in there tonight. Leave the door open so if Edward fusses you may hear him."

"You are very thoughtful. It is kind of you, my lord."

"There is much I would do if I could." He said nothing more on that score. He left the room shortly, his place taken by a demure maid. She was sister to a Fairfax Hall groom and known by Claudia to be a sensible girl.

On her way down to join the others, Claudia took time to examine the house. She had flown up the stairs earlier. Now she had a few moments in which to admire the beautiful, if simple, style of the house. Admirable, indeed! Lord Hawke was to be praised for not decimating his inheritance. Any woman would be delighted to reign here!

Dinner proved a pleasant, although brief, break.

Claudia reassured Olivia and Adela that all would be well. "It is merely for one night and I am certain that even the vicar and Mrs. Alcock would approve my remaining with Edward since he is not to be moved until tomorrow." She raised her brows at Adela.

"Mrs. Logan will see to it that a maid is nearby?"

"I have not the slightest worry," Claudia said with an inward sigh. This was too true. Lord Hawke had kept his distance from her quite easily. She would be as safe as can be.

When she returned to Edward's bedside, she found him restless and fretful. "It hurts, Mama," he whimpered.

Beemish had left a potion to give him. She sent the maid down for fresh water, then administered the medicine. Within a short time, Edward fell into a healing sleep.

It was very late when the door cracked open and Lord Hawke slipped into the room. "How is he?" he whispered.

"Sleeping." Her weary response brought him to her side.

He drew her to her feet. "And so should you. Allow me to sit with him a bit, then I will summon the maid. We can take turns. Go now, you will be better able to manage then."

His voice and manner were so kind Claudia had to blink back tears of fatigue and worry. She swayed, only to be caught in his arms. She gave him a half smile and found herself pulled against his firm body. It was such a comfort to lean on his shoulder. She alone had been responsible for Edward this past year, although even when his father was alive only she oversaw his care. He came first. Perhaps it might be a good thing for him to be in a school? Yet he seemed so vulnerable. How could she?

Hawke felt the tremors that shook the slim form nestled against him. How ironic. He wanted this woman in his arms, in his life, but not quite like this. He carefully placed a hand at her back. When she simply sighed and settled against him, he wrapped his other arm around her, pulling her closer. He was merely offering comfort, he told himself.

She drew back, shook her head, and gazed up at him. The lone candle offered a soft golden light. "Thank you. I rarely receive comfort anymore."

Hawke knew he shouldn't—yet he must. Giving her a chance to pull away should she oppose him, he slowly lowered his head and claimed her lips. It was not a sensual kiss. Rather it was one of compassion, longing, caring. He felt as though they were as one. He stroked her back like he might have done to a child.

Just as desires began to rouse and his control began to slip, she stepped away, breaking the bond that had united them.

She stared at him for long moments, then glanced at her stepson. "I will get some sleep. I am not myself, I think. Have the maid wake me in two hours."

"Three." Hawke let her go, knowing there was tomorrow.

Chapter Eleven

*C*laudia awoke with a start. She had been dreaming, a truly vivid dream. He could not truly have comforted her, kissed her as he had, could he? It must be her imagination. But upon opening her eyes, it all came back to her. She was at Hawke's Rest with Edward in the adjacent room recovering from his broken arm.

And the owner of this elegant pile had indeed kissed her, comforted her in his arms. She had not imagined it, nor could she invent her reaction. She very much feared that she had kissed him back, not to forget melting against him in a most audacious manner. His kiss had turned her bones to jelly, set her blood on fire, and totally shaken her to her toes. This was how he comforted?

And this time, she doubted he would dub that kiss as one from a spinster! However, she did have to wonder what his kiss might be like if he was set on wooing her. The very image was inconceivable. It was also a thing she should put far from her mind. This was a handsome London gentleman. He was able to pick a wife from the highest *ton*, should he wish to marry. Unless . . . he had another position in mind for Claudia?

In an instant she was on her feet, thrusting her arms into the silly robe that Adela insisted she accept. Adela's notion of a gift for her hostess was very unusual! It was a frivolous affair with lavender ribbon adorning a charming lavender print of sumptuous silk with masses of fragile lace trim. She hurried into the room where Edward was ensconced in that massive bed, belting the robe as she went. And she abruptly halted.

Lord Hawke sprawled in a chair beside the bed, seemingly sound asleep, his head pillowed on his arms that rested on the bed.

Seeing that Edward still slept, she quietly pivoted to return to her small sanctuary. She certainly did not wish Lord Hawke to see her in this slightly scandalous attire.

"You are awake so early?" The rich voice sounded a trifle rough, as though he needed to clear his throat.

Claudia froze, her hand outstretched to the doorknob. She half turned to peer at Lord Hawke. He stretched and covered a yawn. Dear heaven, did the man have to look so utterly marvelous when awakened after an interrupted night? If he were a sweet, he would have been consumed in an instant.

"I am not given—as a rule—to being a slugabed." Drat! Did her voice have to sound so breathless? The last thing she desired was to have Lord Hawke know how he affected her. *That* was something she was reluctant to admit to herself.

"Edward was a trifle fussy in the last part of the night. I sent the maid to her room and took over. You needed your sleep after yesterday. I know it must have been difficult for you." When Claudia would have spoken, Hawke held up a hand. "No, no, it is no more than I ought to do, considering he tumbled from the pony *I* gave him in *my* stable yard—a result from the stupid dog belonging to one of *my* tenants."

While he spoke, he rose and strolled around the bed until he reached her side. She flushed under his regard, her hand coming up to brush back her unruly curls. Her dainty embroidered nightcap had come off while she slept and now her hair tumbled about her shoulders. It had been years since any man had seen her hair without benefit of a day cap. She took a step away from him. It wasn't easy, for she was drawn to him. Foolish girl! She stood her ground while she wondered what would be next. What a pity her feet refused to cooperate and return her to the adjacent dressing room.

"It was not your fault, and you know it." She would at least insist upon this.

He shook his head. Then he reached out to touch her hair where it trailed down the front of her robe— that silly confection of clothing. It was as though he could resist her no more than she could withstand him. Nervous, she nibbled at her lower lip, wondering how best to retreat. It was the sensible thing to do and she had been sensible for years.

Hawke studied the vision before him. Her dark lashes looked to owe nothing to the judicious use of elderberries or burnt cork. Her delicate skin was flushed with sleep—or an awareness of him perhaps? He could not recall ever seeing a more delicious delight in morning attire. The confection she wore ought to bring an award to the woman who designed it. And her hair? Spun gold might come close, but lack the glimmer, the lustrous sheen. He longed to thread his fingers through those strands, to touch that satin skin. Last night had proved she did not kiss like a spinster. In fact . . . he wanted more.

"Thank you for your kindness last evening," she said, breaking into his wayward thoughts. "I felt the weight of being a stepmother. So much depends on that little boy." She gazed on the sleeping lad with warmth that Hawke envied.

Then she looked at him again. She was recalling that kiss. He knew it. He could see the sensual awareness flare in her eyes. He doubted if he would or could ever forget it. He had begun his embrace as a comfort, for she had looked so tired, so lost. He ought to have known it would escalate into something far more. The joy of it was that she had responded so totally.

He took a step toward her, desiring to recapture those sensations again, the feel of her in his arms, her mouth against his, that spiraling wonder.

"Mama," Edward whimpered.

Hawke ran his hand over the stubble of his unshaven chin and shook his head. What an idiot he was, to be so completely lost in the rare beauty before him that he forgot the boy.

Claudia immediately went to her stepson's side, sinking down on the edge of that immense bed, her frivolous robe cascading around her and creating a silken lavender print and lace pool. "What is it, love?"

Hawke envied the lad her tender solicitude, the gentle touch of her hand. He would have to tuck the memory of her lavender and lace confection away in a corner of his mind for later appreciation. "I'll see you in a while," he murmured before slipping from the room.

"I hurt." Edward's face crumpled with pain. He looked about to cry.

Ever so gently Claudia eased him up from the bed and into her lap, taking care not to bump his arm. "You may have a little toast and tea if you like. Later on we shall go home."

He settled against her, rubbing his face against the silken robe, fingering the lavish lace with his free hand. "I like this. You should wear it a lot."

"Lady Dunston presented it to me. It's a robe for wearing in the bedroom." Claudia hoped Lord Hawke would forget she had been so improperly garbed. Likely it was too much to expect. Those eyes took note and he seemed to remember everything.

Edward held out the bandaged arm to examine it. "This is very stiff. Can I get up now? I think it might not hurt so much if I do not have to stay in bed."

"That can be so tiresome, can't it? We shall see what can be done for you. Cousin Olivia brought some clean clothes over for us. I wonder what she brought for you?" Claudia set him down on the comfortable chair vacated by Lord Hawke.

It took some time and a bit of cleverness to get Edward into some clothing. The skeleton suit was a problem until she had the idea of cutting open the left sleeve. After that it was relatively simple. Stockings and sturdy boots were donned and he was ready for his breakfast.

"If you can sit here a bit, I believe you will find a dandy book to look at. I must change. I can't go to breakfast in my nightgown!" She pretended horror at the mere thought.

Edward giggled as intended. Leaving him with something to look at, Claudia whipped into the little adjacent room and hurried into the garments that Olivia brought last night. While there was not a thing wrong with the blue sprigged muslin, Claudia hadn't worn anything so frivolous for over a year. It was a trifle out of date, but Claudia doubted if anyone—and by that she meant Lord Hawke—would notice.

When she returned to the bedroom it was to find Lord Hawke sitting with Edward on his lap. They were looking at pictures with Edward making comments.

Claudia halted at the end of the bed. "I, er, that is, I am grateful to you for your hospitality, sir. I thought we might depart after breakfast. If that is agreeable with you?"

"I would have liked to have the sensible Beemish look him over first. Do you think that his arm is just a touch swollen? The bandage seems rather snug for him."

Alarmed, Claudia went to where the pair sat and dropped to her knees to examined the bandage. "I cannot tell. It doesn't look swollen. Edward, does it hurt dreadfully?"

He shook his head. She observed how he leaned against Lord Hawke, so trusting and confident. A glance at Hawke's face told her that he was unaccustomed to little boys in his lap. Yet he did very well. She could almost imagine him sitting with a child of his own, two dark heads bending over a book.

"Toast and tea, I believe. Then when we are home again, we can hope Mr. Beemish will give us a good report." Claudia rose to her feet, wondering if she ought to take Edward from Hawke.

"It will mean six weeks in that stiff bandage at the very least," Hawke cautioned.

"I suppose so. Yet I think this lightweight strapping will be so much better than a heavy wooden splint."

"I could play with my boat when that channel is done," Edward said with a touch of cunning. "I promise not to get the bandage dirty."

Claudia laughed at this piece of nonsense. "I think little boys and dirt are drawn together. But we will slip some fabric over that bandage and hope to keep it dry and clean if we can."

Hawke stared at the laughing face so close to his. Never had he seen skin so clear, so luminous. How was he to endure?

Taking a stoic breath, he rose with Edward in his arms, letting the book slide to the floor. Claudia picked it up to replace on the table. "Breakfast. I don't know about you two, but tea and toast, plus a few other things sounds rather good about now." Hawke started for the door.

"I think I am hungry," Edward cried in surprise.

Claudia chuckled, then opened the door so they might all go down to the morning room where there was certain to be an assortment of pastries and fruit, possibly an egg.

She found everything waiting for them. A bowl of steaming oatmeal topped with raisins and sprinkled with sugar was set before Edward at once. It was a

dish he adored and he poured rich cream over the
cereal, commenting it was a good thing his left arm
was the one that broke, not his right.

Hawke had deposited Edward, glanced at Claudia,
then took his place at the head of the table. Earlier
his garb had been what a man might don for an emer-
gency. Claudia had thought it rather endearing—his
tousled hair, the rumpled shirt hastily pulled over his
head, sans waistcoat and cravat. His shirt had been
tucked into a pair of gray trousers. It was hardly the
attire of the fashionable Lord Hawke. And yet she
had found him far more approachable in that crumpled garb, perhaps too much so! It was as well he was
now the ultimate perfection of a London gentleman.
No tousled hair, no rumpled shirt.

Lords Elliot and Pace, followed by Mr. Lodge straggled into the morning room to partake of a hearty
breakfast.

Edward watched with wide brown eyes as each man
piled his plate high with food. He polished off his
beloved oatmeal, then asked Claudia if he might have
something more. "An egg, a bit of sausage, some
toast," he began.

"You need strength to heal that arm, lad," Mr.
Lodge said with an amazingly solemn face.

"Indeed you do," added Lord Pace. He turned to
Claudia to ask, "I gather you will go back to Fairfax
Hall later this morning. Would it be agreeable to you
if we came over this afternoon? The boy might enjoy
a bit of company."

Mr. Lodge nodded. "Those soldiers and cannon can
be tricky to set up."

Lord Elliot cleared his throat. "I imagine Lady
Dunston might be willing to supervise the launching
of a toy boat once that raised channel is finished. You
think it might be ready by this afternoon?"

Rather astounded at this barrage of enthusiasm for
visiting a small boy, Claudia nodded. "I feel he would

be extremely pleased to have such elevated company. And I believe that at least part of the raised channel should be done." She gave Edward a bemused look, knowing better than to ruffle his hair, something he detested. Instead she merely patted his shoulder. "Would you like the gentlemen to come after you have a bit of rest to recover from the trip home?"

"I won't need a nap, Mama. I am a very big boy, you know."

"I know. I did suggest a mere rest."

"We shall all ride over this afternoon. It will offer Edward a pleasant diversion." Hawke gave a pointed look at his friends. Something was conveyed in that expression for they all smiled, although all that was heard were murmurs of agreement.

Conversation became general. The weather was touched on, the prospect of rain considered. Then Lord Hawke cleared his throat. "I believe it would be best if we take Edward home in my landau. There would be ample room so you needn't fear additional injury to his arm."

"I am sure that a carriage from Fairfax could be sent for, my lord." She did not wish to be beholden to him for more than utterly necessary.

He inhaled sharply. "Woman, allow me to make amends how I can. We will take the landau."

She recognized the tone of exasperation in his voice as that of a man not to be crossed. "Thank you," she said in a meek little voice she thought might placate him. She almost smiled at the look he gave her. So he was suspicious of her timid tone? Well, and so he ought to be. She compressed her lips, knowing it might not be the best thing to grin at this point.

Following a hearty breakfast—at least for all the males—Claudia went up to the room she and Edward had used to find the maid had everything neatly folded and ready to go.

As she went down the stairs, her small case in hand,

she took the time to look about her again. What an admirable house, to be sure! Everything was well polished, the Turkish rugs gleamed in the morning sun, brasses sparkled, and portraits were free of dust. Handsome they were too. If they were ancestors, they were a fine-looking lot.

"Aunt Celestine is the prettiest of the group," Lord Hawke said as he strolled to where she paused on the next to the bottom step. "Uncle George is the dragon on the end and Great-uncle Herbert is that chap with the beard."

"An admirable collection, to be sure," she replied.

"My father is in the library. Come see what you think." He relieved her of the little case, setting it on a hall chair.

Without waiting for an answer, he casually took her elbow to guide her, not that she needed it. She let his hand be, though. His touch gave her a warmth she had lacked for quite some time—if she had ever known such.

The portrait over the fireplace was as one might expect. She was surprised that it hung in this house, as hadn't she been told that Lord Hawke possessed other estates? Most likely he owned a house in London as well.

"Your father favored this particular house?" she queried. The son strongly resembled his parent. He had the same blue eyes with that intense, romantic hint in them and the same rich brown hair. The artist had captured a fine, almost alive expression.

"This house is the one that caused him the least trouble. My own portrait is in the London house. My mother's is there as well. The other houses have landscapes and my mother's flower paintings."

"Your mother painted?" Claudia was delighted to learn they had a common interest, even though she'd never meet the lady.

"She still does. I will show you them when you visit the other houses."

Since Claudia had no intention of visiting his other estates, she merely smiled and let that comment pass. It wasn't that she wouldn't like to visit them. A lady simply didn't enter a gentleman's home without a chaperon or an exceedingly good reason. She knew of none.

"I imagine Edward is anxious to return to Fairfax Hall," he said as he walked with her toward the door. "I requested the carriage be brought around shortly. Will that be agreeable with you?"

"Of course." Claudia wanted to say more. Actually, she wanted him to kiss her again but a lady did not make that sort of a request. Resolute, she turned away from the appealing library and its owner to find Edward.

"I wish you might stay a little longer. I worry that you are moving Edward too soon."

"Oh, I could not!" She gave him a troubled look. Why did his voice have such a bewitching quality to it? And why didn't her feet want to go to Edward? Wicked woman!

"Lady Fairfax?" Mr. Lodge paused in the doorway. "I believe the carriage is here. Would it be agreeable if we all rode along with you? On our horses, of course. I think Edward would enjoy an escort home." His face wore a hopeful expression.

Claudia thought that Olivia would be much in evidence if Mr. Lodge were to come. Thinking it would be a good idea to encourage the connection and put a spoke in the vicar's metaphoric wheel, Claudia gave the gentleman a warm smile. "Edward would be thrilled for such a fine escort. Although I fancy Olivia will be surprised to see you."

Mr. Lodge looked enormously pleased and left them at once, heading up to his room.

•

"Was that necessary?" Lord Hawke gave her a cool stare.

Good grief, the man sounded piqued! Claudia gave him an affronted glare. "I accepted his offer in the spirit in which it was given, my lord." She whisked herself from the library, marching down the hall to where Edward lingered at his breakfast.

Hawke watched her sail down the hall and disappear around the corner. He was going to have to guard his tongue and remember the other men had other interests. He was becoming obsessed with Lady Fairfax and there was no indication that she felt one way or the other about him.

It took but a brief time to settle Edward on the well-cushioned seat of the landau. Since the day was fine, the top had been lowered. There was ample room for Claudia to sit by him. Her little case reposed on the floor with an empty seat across from them.

She gave Hawke a challenging look, quite as though she dared him to take the place opposite. He smiled, then mounted Kismet, riding up to the side of the carriage with a flourish. She had the look of one who has had a treat taken away from her. He guessed she had intended to be very aloof and prim. He chuckled.

"I am pleased you can laugh upon our departure," she said in an overly gracious manner. "I would be distressed to think we had been too great a burden on your hospitality."

"I did say I wished you might stay longer," he reminded.

"Yes, well, I think it good for Edward to be at home." She had floundered there for a moment.

The others rode up, cutting off anything else either Hawke or Claudia might have said.

Lord Hawke spoke to his coachman, then pulled back so the carriage might proceed. Claudia leaned back against the squabs, enjoying the luxurious feel of them against her back.

"This is a very fine carriage, Mama. I think Lord Hawke has a very fine house as well. It is as fine as mine."

Claudia froze, her hand suspended in midair. She slowly brought it to her lap as she mulled over Edward's words. Of course Fairfax Hall was his. She knew that. He had reminded her that her days were numbered there. She had ample time to fix up the dower house, but she might as well get on with it. The years flew by so fast and before she knew it Edward would be at Oxford as his father had wished. And then he would marry.

"I will be eight before long. How long will this bandage need to be on my arm?"

Claudia automatically informed him, reassuring him that Beemish would take the greatest care of him and his injury.

Since word had been sent that Edward was coming this morning, Olivia and Adela awaited them on the front steps as the carriage made its way up the last of the avenue. Dorothy Cork lingered in the background. Evidently her parents had granted permission for her to stay at the Hall. One more person to entertain the invalid. Lord Pace would be enormously pleased.

The hubbub of arrival with the various people greeting one another and Mrs. Tibbins exclaiming over her favorite's great white bandage masked Claudia's silence.

"My lady," Mrs. Tibbins inserted at a quiet moment, "how shall we deal with Master Edward? I fancy he will like to rest just a bit, perhaps on the chaise longue in the sitting room?"

"The very thing!" Claudia spoke quietly but was heard.

She was about to gather Edward into her arms when

Hawke gently picked her up and set her aside. He capably handled Edward as though dealing with small boys was second nature to him. The others parted to permit him passage into the house.

Claudia meekly followed, seething that he could so easily set her to the side. Just picked her up like a post. That she still tingled where his hands had rested so intimately on her waist was not the point here.

Precisely what was the point was lost when they entered the sitting room. The rocking horse had been brought down as had the magnificent set of soldiers Adela had brought him. The room looked like his nursery!

"Oh, dear." Claudia put a hand to her lips in dismay.

"Mama, isn't this famous? I can stay here with you while you paint and my favorite toys will be with me."

Hawke set Edward on the chaise longue, allowing Claudia to tuck pillows behind the boy for support. He could lean back to rest, yet could see everything going on about him. It was far preferable to being tucked away in his room.

"I can only hope he doesn't try to do too much," Claudia whispered to Lord Hawke at her side. The glance he gave her might be considered tender. She had not received such in the past so she wasn't certain.

"Someone will be in here all day, and at night I know you will have help." A half smile warmed his face.

"Thank you for all you have done for Edward. I appreciate it." She prudently took a step back while she faced him.

"It was my pleasure, I assure you." His eyes reminded her that she had enjoyed a certain pleasure as well.

Chapter Twelve

*M*r. Beemish proclaimed himself pleased with the arrangements for Edward. "I have observed that it isn't good to keep a child bed bound in a case like this. An active boy would only pine away. I know you will find a way to keep him quiet and occupied." His eyes sparkled from beneath bushy brows.

Claudia wondered if the dear man had ever attempted to keep a nearly eight-year-old boy amused and quietly occupied for any time. Now that the pain was lessening, Edward demanded more diversions. She was soon weary from trying to entertain him. She urged the workmen to complete the stone fence that would have a channel atop it so Edward might amuse himself with a boat and remain clean—or relatively so. It was impossible to keep a boy from soiling his clothing completely.

When the four men arrived that afternoon she was more than glad to see them. That Olivia, Adela, and Dorothy would apply themselves either to entertain the gentlemen or help keep Edward occupied mattered little. He would be kept busy merely watching all the others.

"He slept a bit, but now thinks he ought to be doing everything he enjoys." She hadn't reached the end of her wits, but it wouldn't take long before she did at the rate he was going.

"Why can't I . . ." began Edward's every other sentence.

Mr. Lodge, with an admiring Olivia at his side, and Lord Pace, with Dorothy Cork to oversee, set out the array of soldiers and all the other pieces that Adela had brought. Lord Elliot sketched a sort of background of mountains and terrain that would have been seen in Spain. Edward insisted he wanted nothing less than a Spanish battle scene.

"You will have your hands full, my dear," Hawke murmured to Claudia while they watched the others at work.

"I cannot leave him to his nanny. She has enough with keeping him settled at night."

"So you realized that you cannot burn your candle at both ends, did you?" He glanced at her before turning his attention to the battle scene being created.

"I shall take care, my lord." Claudia gave him a wary look, then offered Edward a cup of chamomile tea brought by a solicitous Mrs. Tibbins. He had been too excited to eat much lunch. She hoped to tempt him with small sandwiches and perhaps a few biscuits.

"Sir," Edward inserted into the quiet conversation, "did Mama show you my dragon?"

Hawke shook his head. "She hasn't had time, my boy."

Claudia knew better than to refuse. That dratted man would simply search her desk until he found the design. With an air of resignation she dug through the papers on her little desk and came up with the whimsical dragon drawing. She rather liked the impish dragon, his fanciful tail curving so as to fit the curve of the plate.

"It looks as though it grins. Have you ever *seen* a grinning dragon, my dear?" Hawke inquired from far too close to her.

"Actually, I haven't seen any dragon—at least a four-footed one," she amended.

"Ah, so it is only fairies you see at the bottom of your garden." His voice was innocent enough, but she could see amusement lurking in those blue eyes of his.

If he enjoyed baiting her and found pleasure in it, she wouldn't quibble. As long as there were others around she thought she could keep him in place. She would take care not to be alone with him. That way lay danger. As Olivia had predicted, Hawke was a dangerous man, at least to Claudia's peace of mind!

The new footman from Hawke's Rest entered the room, seeking Claudia at once. "A shipment has come from Bristol, my lady. Says Worcester on the crate."

"My white china! I do hope nothing has been broken in transport." Turning to Edward she added, "Now I shall have the plate for your dragon. You may watch me paint it if you like."

Ignoring the others, she slipped from the room to hurry to where the large wooden crate sat in the entry hall. The footman had been correct in assuming she would not wish this box in the kitchen.

He pried the lid from the top for her. She carefully began sifting through the wood shavings, removing one piece of china at a time. She examined each plate with care, checking for flaws or cracks. She nearly dropped a plate when Hawke came up behind her and spoke.

"All satisfactory so far?"

"*Please* do not creep up on me like that," she cried in vexation. "I nearly dropped this plate."

"You intend to work in the sitting room? With Edward to observe you? How can you keep him entertained if you are concentrating on painting?"

Claudia pressed her lips together in irritation. She knew how difficult it would be to keep Edward amused. "Perhaps he will enjoy watching his dragon take form and color. Once it is fired he can have his plate at meals."

Hawke picked up a plate, turning it over to look

at the back. "Royal Worcester? Not bad quality, I must say."

"It does well." Thinking to pacify him with a modicum of information, she added, "A man in Bristol orders what I wish and when he receives his own order, sends mine on to me. I get a better price that way."

He made no comment on her economy. She saw no reason to enlighten him as to why she was careful with what she spent. Oh, her quarterly income was adequate as long as she didn't indulge herself too much in china and other nonsense.

"What is all this?" Adela inquired, having left the sitting room to see what went on. Lord Elliot gazed over her shoulder.

"My white china for painting." The others came to look as well, and it was but minutes before Edward called out demanding to join them.

Before Claudia could explain why he couldn't come, Hawke had slipped into the sitting room to pick up the lad, returning with him in a trice.

"That is a very nice plate, Mama. Will you paint it for me?" Edward's wide-eyed smile was wistfully luminous.

Claudia smiled. "Of course I will. I'll do anything you wish—within reason, that is." She tacked on the last at the gleam that lit Lord Hawke's eyes. She would not tolerate any sly comments with Edward, not to forget all the others, around.

He knew it, too.

Two by two the others drifted back to the sitting room to leave Hawke, Claudia, and Edward by the clutter of wood shavings and a tidy stack of china.

"I won't have to wonder where you are or what you are doing now," Lord Hawke observed, the gleam still lurking in his eyes.

"I cannot imagine why you would be the slightest

interested in how I might spend my days. No one else is," Claudia retorted.

"Edward," Hawke said in a musing way, "what can we do to let your mama know we care what happens to her?"

Edward gave that a bit of thought, then said, "I would order her a new dress from London. Maybe three. A blue one for certain, perhaps a pretty green one, and maybe a pink? I like blue best of all, though."

Claudia was dumbfounded at this. "Why, Edward, I had no idea you were aware of what I wore."

"I heard Lady Dunston say it was time you got out of blacks and into something pretty. So I would order something pretty." His brown eyes were merry, quite as though he knew he bordered on what would be improper for a gentleman to say.

"Lady Dunston would have me travel to London merely to order up a wardrobe. Utter nonsense." Claudia busied herself with digging out more china, far too aware that Hawke had heard all and stared at her too intently.

Hawke gave Claudia a searching look. "Quarter day too distant?"

"If I choose to spend on china rather than frivolous garments, that is my option. Is it not?" she demanded. Lord Hawke was being a trifle presumptuous. While it was true that she had not really spent more than she ought to, the cost of all the china meant that she would be reluctant to order an entire wardrobe of the latest design.

"You need clothes, however." His gaze roamed over her form in a far too familiar manner.

Swallowing her ire, she gave him a grim smile. "Perhaps I will order a gown or two. Madame Clotilde has my measurements. That was one thing Basil insisted upon when we married. Later, she made my mourning clothes." There—with one neat sentence Claudia reminded his lordship that she was a recent widow with a reputation to uphold. "I plan to remain in half mourning a bit longer." She didn't know why she had added that. She hadn't meant to, that was certain. What was it about Lord Hawke that led her into saying words she hadn't meant to say?

Without saying a word in reply he left her, Edward still in his arms, returning to the sitting room where he was met with cries urging him to inspect all that had been done.

Claudia stood holding a plate to her bosom, staring after Hawke with a sensation of loss. Well, she did *not* seek a closer relationship with Lord Hawke. And if she believed that nonsense she deserved to find the rest of the china in bits and pieces.

Mrs. Tibbins breezed into the entryway with a large tray. She began to stack the plates that had been uncrated. "If you would like to return to your guests, madam, I shall finish this dusty job for you."

Claudia almost laughed. Well, she was neatly informed that she was not only neglecting her callers, she was becoming rather dirty in the process. "As you please. When you call me 'madam' like that, I know I am perilously near to disgrace."

"Never that, my lady. I do know, however, that you want to do what is best for Miss Olivia and Master Edward. I fancy Lady Dunston and Miss Cork can manage well on their own."

"You do not think the vicar will come today, do you?" Claudia whispered in horror.

"It would be well to cement whatever is blooming between Miss Olivia and Mr. Lodge before that vicar can spoil her chances. Vicar Woodley sees only to his own interests. Does he know Miss Olivia has a tidy inheritance?"

Claudia shook her head, utterly bemused at this spate of loquaciousness from her housekeeper.

"See that he doesn't learn of it. Bad enough that pushing parson thinks to dip his fingers into your money pot."

"Mrs. Tibbins, I do believe you are a jewel, even if you exceed what is proper just a little. I shall go to my guests, make certain Mr. Lodge and Olivia are together, and keep a weather eye on Edward. I do not want him to get overtired."

"Send them outside looking for twigs and moss for that scene they are setting up for Edward. Seems to me they are having a right jolly time of it. Wonder if the boy will get a chance to play at all!" She brushed aside some wood shavings, then placed another plate on the tray.

Chuckling to herself, Claudia marched down to the sitting room, pausing at the door to survey who was doing what, and with whom. It was an interesting sight.

Olivia and Mr. Lodge were arranging some hills Olivia had crafted from wrapping paper. On the other side Adela and Lord Elliot set up the cannon and other accessories. Looking around, she found Dorothy Cork and Lord Pace deep in a discussion on horses, or at least it appeared that way from where she stood.

Edward had fallen asleep on the chaise longue. He wore a contented look on his face and she intended to leave him be.

"You wish me to carry him up to his room?" Hawke murmured at her side.

"Mercy, you do frighten a body with your stealing up so quietly. As to Edward, leave him be. Obviously the noise lulled him to sleep and he would only wake up if you move him."

"Seems quite sensible."

"I am quite sensible on occasion," Claudia replied.

"I prefer the moments when you forget."

She gave him a wary glance before slipping a light shawl over Edward. "I shall request tea, if you think the others can abandon the project long enough." Her lips curved in a smile at the sight of the adults having such a marvelous time playing with a little boy's toys.

"They will need some sustenance before long. Tea, seed cake, scones, perhaps watercress sandwiches . . . you know what they like." Hawke seemed amused at the preoccupation of the others.

"I gather you enjoy watercress sandwiches? I prefer egg and cress, myself." She turned to the door, intent upon speaking with Mrs. Tibbins.

"Egg and cress are excellent. Another thing we have in common, my dear." He stared at her in a most disconcerting manner that sent a tremor up her spine.

She gave him a sharp stare at his words. "I was not aware that we *ought* to have things in common, my lord."

His face was altogether too bland for her ease. "Well, we are Edward's guardians, are we not?"

"That is no reason, and you know it. I hear stories of dreadful guardians who quarrel over the slightest thing."

"All the more reason for us to be united." His thoughts beyond that were concealed behind his mild expression.

Claudia had the impression that more was contained in his simple sentences than she was catching. She dare not ask him what he meant by his words. That would be offering him an opening that she might regret.

"Excuse me. I must see Mrs. Tibbins." Without waiting for an answer, she whisked herself to the entry hall where Mrs. Tibbins removed what had to be the last plate from near the bottom of the crate.

"Nothing broken, my lady. The china was that well packed."

"Good. Would you please arrange one of your splendid teas for us? I wouldn't be surprised if all that creative activity has made my friends hungry." She half turned, then added, "Lord Hawke desires some egg and cress sandwiches if you can manage it. Seed cake and scones as well. That should give you an idea of his hunger."

"Not all he desires, though. Not by a long shot," the housekeeper murmured as she marched down the hall to the kitchen.

Really, Mrs. Tibbins overstepped herself too often. It would be impossible to replace her, however. Besides, she always meant well and she doted on Edward. No doubt there would be a few special gingerbread biscuits on the tray as well as the rest of the food requested. It never ceased to amaze her how between them, Cook and Mrs. Tibbins could whip up just what was wanted.

"Egg and cress coming up shortly, my lord," Claudia quietly reported to Lord Hawke upon reentering the sitting room.

"I had no doubt you would manage. Basil was a fool, you know. He did not appreciate all he had here."

Claudia stiffened, her face freezing as it was wont to do when anyone was so gauche as to mention her late husband.

"Don't pucker up on me like you just ate a sour pickle. I know what he was and most of what he did. If I say he was a fool it is because I know it to be a fact."

Claudia turned her head away so Hawke couldn't see her eyes. She had tears in them and the last thing she wanted was to have Hawke see her all weepy. She gave a proud toss of her head before walking away from him to the window. From it she could view her favorite part of the garden she had created. Diligent work there had taken her mind off all the other problems that plagued her over the past few years.

"So. You will order a few gowns for the coming winter season. A green velvet gown for Christmas, I believe. Now that is settled and a very fine idea it is, too." He thrust a crisp square of white linen into her hands, although said nothing about mopping up possible tears.

"I never said . . ." she snapped, her feelings having been trod on so recently. She accepted the linen and prudently dried her eyes. Resolutely, she continued to stare out of the window.

"Edward wants you to have them. I have observed that whatever Edward wants of you, he gets. It is a weapon I intend to use when necessary." His voice was still rich and deep, yet he had that hateful assurance in it that she knew guaranteed him what *he* wanted.

She was saved from a reply to this rather dangerous topic by the entrance of Mrs. Tibbins and a maid with all necessary for a splendid tea. The only thing Claudia could think was that the cook had looked at the kitchen clock and known tea would be required momentarily.

"Ah, the joys of a well-run household," Hawke murmured in her ear. "You will make an excellent wife, my dear."

With that amazing remark he left her side to join the others now clustered around the tea tray. Claudia hastened to join them and began pouring tea and dispensing the tasty tidbits. She tucked the peculiar comment in the back of her mind to be examined later.

Gingerbread biscuits had been piled on a small plate, just the size to please Edward. He awoke and politely demanded his favorite treat.

"It is a good thing that boy is so easily pleased or he would be quite spoiled," Adela commented to Claudia before she moved to join Lord Elliot.

Spoiled? Well, the poor lad had been dealt one blow after another—losing his mother, then his father. Fortunately, Claudia thought that no word of his half sisters had reached his ears. Knowing Edward, he'd insist on meeting them! But it was a simple matter to cosset him a bit. He was such an endearing boy.

Following tea, the group returned to creating a scene worthy of the splendid assortment of soldiers, horses, cannons and all the other accessories Adela had bought.

"We need moss for shrubs, I should think. Those we found in Spain were not much like proper English bushes," Lord Elliot explained to Edward.

"Was it a dreary place?" the boy asked.

"Part of the year when there wasn't much rain. Dreadful heat, as I recall," Elliot replied.

"I hadn't realized you fought in Spain during the war," Adela said, standing closely to his side while they arranged moss. "I am glad you came through it unscathed."

He gazed down into Adela's gray eyes with what appeared to Claudia to be tender regard. She hastily looked elsewhere, not wishing to intrude on something personal.

Claudia wandered over to see what Mr. Lodge and Olivia were doing. They were so well matched that Claudia decided the vicar didn't stand a chance with Olivia, even if he did discover the tidy inheritance she was to receive upon her marriage. She was behind them in the somewhat noisy room when she heard quiet words that gave her pause.

"And he said that if he needed to get that land, he would just marry her." Mr. Lodge chuckled softly. "It is cheaper than buying it. And then—she might not be willing to sell." He bowed his head over whatever it was he worked on.

Olivia, obviously intent on what Mr. Lodge was doing, replied, "He cannot be certain Claudia would marry him. He may *have* to offer to buy the land she now owns."

"Well, knowing Hawke, he always gets what he wants."

Whatever else they might have said was lost as Claudia slipped away at that point.

Could it be true that the real reason that Lord Hawke paid her attention was to get his hands on that strip of land that had come to her on Basil's death? She had learned the history of the property. It had once belonged to the Hawke title. Some Lord Hawke had in the past gambled it away to Basil's ancestor. She didn't see why she should hand it over to the present Lord Hawke, even if she got a good price for it. But if she married him, it would automatically be his.

"A problem, my dear?" Lord Hawke said, a quizzical expression on his handsome face. Those blue eyes were more intense than ever as he peered at her face.

"I am not your dear," she reminded. "Nor do I think I will ever be your dear, if that is in your mind." With that pithy statement, she turned away from Hawke to seek out Dorothy and Lord Pace.

Hawke stood where she left him, somewhat stunned. There had been obvious pique that bordered on dislike in her eyes and manner. What in the world had happened? Why had she so abruptly glared at him as though he were detestable? He would have to get to the bottom of the mystery before he could pursue the widow further, that much was certain.

Somehow the group found themselves agreeing that the afternoon had been delightful and now little Edward needed quiet and rest. Within short order the gentlemen had mounted their steeds and were cantering down the avenue on their way to Hawke's Rest. The women tidied up the military scene that had been created, then went up to their rooms.

Adela returned to the sitting room in a few minutes, seeking Claudia. "What happened? Your face was far too pale for it to be merely fatigue."

Drawing her friend away from the chaise longue where Edward now snoozed, Claudia shook her head.

"It is merely a small surprise, that is all. I ought to have expected it, I imagine. People can be so deceiving."

"I assume you speak of Lord Hawke. No one else would affect you so." Adela walked at Claudia's side to the far end of the room where Edward could not possibly overhear them if he woke.

"Silly me. I was beginning to think he rather liked me. It is humiliating to discover that my company is sought merely because of a strip of land I now possess—a strip of land that Lord Hawke wants. I have been told that he always gets what he wants. Ipso facto, he wants the land I have—it is simple to take me. It makes things so easy. He doesn't even have to purchase it, providing I was willing to sell."

"You don't know that for a fact," Adela said, looking deeply concerned.

"I overheard something not intended for my ears. Mr. Lodge was telling Olivia about it. Surely if Mr. Lodge was so certain of the matter as to tell her, it must be so. He does not seem the gossipy sort."

"No, no, that he does not. Oh, my dear, what a dreadful thing to learn. Quite painful, in fact. Perhaps Mr. Lodge misunderstood something Lord Hawke said. Maybe it was a jest of a kind?" Adela took Claudia's hand, holding it in a comforting clasp. "I will try to learn what I can, if you wish."

"You may try, but I doubt it will be other than this truth. Somehow it all makes sense to me."

Chapter Thirteen

"Let me see. Edward thinks I should order a blue gown, Olivia thinks of almond pink, and someone who shall remain nameless suggested green velvet with Christmas in mind."

Claudia sat at her usually tidy desk, but papers were strewn about and her dragon drawing sat atop a stack of books. She had to keep her mind occupied. It was essential lest her thoughts stray to the words she had overheard yesterday. But why should she be so surprised? Why else would a dashing London peer show interest in her? She was a widow who had not produced a second heir for her first—and most likely only—husband. Every peer wanted an heir and a spare. She was childless.

"May I inquire just why you are in such a stew this morning? It is clear to me that you are upset. What else has happened?" Adela inquired as she entered the sitting room. She had paused at the door, studying her friend with a sapient gaze. "And why is it necessary for you to dither over an order for gowns that truly isn't all that urgent? You always look charming." Adela plumped on the sitting room sofa, a lacy day cap perched atop her elegantly styled hair. As always, she was beautifully garbed. Her eyes saw more than Claudia wished.

"I believe it is a slow time for the London mantua-makers," Claudia replied pensively. "I thought that if I ordered some gowns now my order would receive prompt attention. Besides, I am weary of every dress I own. I didn't order all that many after Basil died. Now they are becoming rather tatty. One must keep up appearances." She flashed a look of defiance at her friend.

"Naturally such an order requires deep thought. Or is there another problem that vexes you?" Adela glanced at the door. No one appeared, nor could any steps be heard on the stairs or in the hall. The house was exceedingly quiet.

Claudia studied her hands, one of which held a fine quill pen. "Well, what I overheard has spun about in my head until I do not know what to do, if anything. Surely he cannot think to marry me merely to possess that strip of land? That seems to me a rather drastic step in view of all that he has . . . not to mention all that he is." She fiddled with the pen, not wishing to reach any conclusions. How foolish, to want to live with an illusion!

"Perhaps you misunderstood, my dear," Adela protested.

"Please, the phrase 'my dear' is one I would rather not hear, even from you. Lord Hawke appears to think I enjoy hearing it, for he uses it frequently when speaking to me." Claudia turned to look fully at Adela. "I mislike speech that means nothing. It seems so empty, so very nonsensical."

"Particularly when you would far rather hear genuine words of love and appreciation?" Adela smiled.

"I would like peace!" Claudia proclaimed stoutly.

"Peace is when things are as they are supposed to be," Adela said thoughtfully. "And unless a few things change a great deal around here, I do not foresee any alteration in a certain gentleman's behavior." She considered her words a few moments, then continued. "I cannot believe Lord Hawke would do such a thing to you. While I understand the land was once part of his estate, surely he could make a decent offer to you to purchase the property? And would you sell?"

Claudia shook her head and sighed. "I do not know. I suppose I ought to ask Mr. Fry, my bailiff, what a fair price might be. I was under the impression that Lord Hawke was beginning to rather like me for myself. Now I shall never know if he is truly attracted to me or that dratted strip of land. Can I trust him?"

"It seems to me that trust is relying completely on someone. He does seem trustworthy, does he not?"

"Appearances can be so deceptive. Although, I confess that he is very good to Edward. I . . . er . . . believe he is kind to animals." Claudia flashed a rueful smile at her friend.

"He is English, my dear. Most Englishmen are kind to animals. In fact, I have read where some men are kinder to their animals than to their wives. Not to say that Lord Hawke would fall into that category. I have heard *nothing* against him."

Steps in the hall terminated the topic, much to Claudia's relief. She wasn't sure if she wished to discuss it anymore. It rather stung her pride to think that a piece of land would tempt a man to woo her, ask her to marry him when he might be inclined elsewhere. How could she tolerate such a marriage!

Mrs. Tibbins bustled into the sitting room, pausing inside the door. "The vicar is come, my lady. Are you to home?"

Claudia exchanged a resigned look with Adela. "Indeed, I am to home, Mrs. Tibbins. You may as well set up a tea tray, for you know how the vicar enjoys your scones." The housekeeper turned to leave and Claudia added, "Oh, say nothing to Miss Greene of his call."

Mrs. Tibbins gave Claudia a knowing nod. "Right you are."

Shortly the vicar strolled into the room, looking

about him as he did to see who was there to impress. "Ah, Lady Fairfax and Lady Dunston! What a lovely day it is. I am surprised to find you here. It is a perfect day for a stroll in the garden."

"By all means, stroll in the garden if you please," Claudia said as sweetly as possible.

She received a confused look from the vicar. "Oh, I see, you are jesting. Now, now, my lady, jesting must be done with great care lest someone misunderstand you."

"I see what you mean," she murmured before turning to the magazine at the side of her desk. She tucked a slip of paper in place before closing it so she would easily find the illustration she liked later on after his nosiness, the vicar, had gone. "One cannot be too careful."

"I am pleased to see my words taken to heart."

Behind him, well out of his sight, Adela raised her gaze to the ceiling in incredulity.

Then he spotted the arrangement of soldiers, the sketched mountain scenery, and the cannons that had been set up the day before. "What is this? It appears to be a game of war!" He quickly turned to face Claudia. "Never say you permit young Lord Fairfax to engage in such a pastime, my lady!"

"I fear I am the guilty one, Vicar Woodley," Adela inserted before Claudia could think of a word to say. "I saw the soldier set in a London shop and thought it might entertain a boy of Edward's age. The gentlemen have been augmenting it as you see."

"As Lord Hawke said to me the other day," Claudia added sweetly, "Edward does not have any little friends with whom he might play, so it is incumbent upon his guardians to find amusements for him. With his broken arm, it is frightfully difficult to think of a pastime that is quiet and absorbing for him. He would far rather be riding his pony or playing on his swing, even mucking about in the stream."

Much to her relief Mrs. Tibbins entered the room with a massive silver tray holding tea, scones, and other assorted dainties. Claudia sent her a look of gratitude. "Thank you, Mrs. Tibbins. Place the tray on that far table." She intended to keep the scones out of the vicar's reach. The pile of scones might be passed—it did not need to serve as his plate!

James, the footman on loan from Hawke, came to the doorway. "The gentlemen are come, my lady. I trust you wish them in here, not in the drawing room?"

"Indeed, James." She met Adela's gaze and forced a smile.

Lord Hawke and Lord Elliot, immediately followed by Lord Pace and Mr. Lodge, walked into the room. Before they had a chance to settle anywhere soft steps were heard on the stairs. Olivia and Dorothy came into the sitting room within minutes. Each gentleman promptly joined the lady who interested him.

Olivia beamed at Mr. Lodge. "What a lovely surprise. The nurserymaid is bringing Edward down shortly. He will be so pleased to find you all here!" Then she caught sight of the vicar. Her mouth opened, but nothing was said.

Claudia almost chuckled at her expression of dismay. It was interesting to see the flush of red that crept up the vicar's face as he beheld his former admirer now at the side of a polished gentleman who would one day inherit from the Earl of Loxley. Claudia could nearly guess his thoughts.

"Er, how pleasant to see you," Olivia said in a tone and manner that gave lie to her words. She was excessively civil.

"Well, the good vicar has come to visit the recovering wounded!" Lord Pace said in a jolly way.

Before the vicar could think of a rejoinder, the maid came in with Edward.

"You carry the lad?" Lord Hawke said in consternation. "It is his arm that is broken, not his foot. Let him walk—as long as he feels able, that is."

Claudia, distinctly annoyed with his lordship, snapped, "He is but a young boy, not some hardy gentleman who wouldn't admit to being injured. There is ample time for him to be moving about on his own." She supposed it might serve Edward better to walk on his own. She erred on the side of caution for he was slight, almost frail. And it was hard to accept Hawke's interference.

"And how do you fare this lovely late summer day, my dear?" Hawke inquired of Claudia, using a patient manner one might use toward a woman who was too obstinate for her own good. "If the workmen have finished the stone wall with the channel at the top perhaps Edward would enjoy sailing this boat?" Lord Hawke strolled over to stand by Claudia, studying her face as though to memorize it. In his hands he held a small boat.

Claudia looked at the boat with dismay. It was magnificent—small but perfect in every aspect. Why, oh why, did this man never put a foot wrong with her stepson?

"Oh," Edward cried with delight. "Mrs. Tibbins told me that it was done and I could try it out later." He slid from the chaise longue where he had been placed and crossed to the side of his guardian. Holding his bandaged arm with proper care, he used his good right hand to examine the boat, meticulously carved in incredible detail. "It is very clever, sir. I think I should like a boat like that some day."

"Well, for now, this one is yours. When you grow up you can decide if you would like a real one of your own."

"Boats are dangerous things," Claudia asserted.

"Not if one is trained to handle them properly. That

is true of a great many things." He stared at her until she knew she blushed. She could feel the heat creeping up her face.

Claudia didn't know how to behave toward Hawke. Had she not overheard those dreadful words, she would act more agreeably toward him. Now all she could think of was her inner hurt that she would be so little valued as to mean nothing more to him than a means to get what he wanted. Well, if that is what he wished, she would just sell him the dratted land. The way things were at present, the land would be of little use to her once Edward could take control of his estate. She could use money to greater effect. Not wishing to reside in the dower house—for that would definitely be too close to Hawke's Rest—she could buy a small place—perhaps in Tunbridge Wells or some other spa. Why, it might even be possible to find another widower who wanted a wife to care for the children of his late wife, she thought, not without a little bitterness.

Evidently Hawke thought he could handle her, if that was what he intended to imply in his words. She decided it was best to simply ignore him. She had observed that seemed to annoy him. Right at the moment there was nothing she wanted more than to annoy that particularly vexing man. And yet . . . He was dashing and handsome, kind, many women's notion of the ideal mate. He kept his possessions in good heart. Everyone liked him. Or, at least, most people. Perhaps the vicar wasn't an admirer even if Lord Hawke generously supported the church.

Wasn't it the most beastly moment to realize that while he didn't seem to want her, other than a means to an end, she wanted him very much, that she had tumbled into love with the last man on earth she ought to love? What a dilemma! She would of necessity go to great lengths to keep him from learning that little detail. He appeared to read her mind with far too much ease. Was she really such an open book? She devoutly hoped not!

He returned to her side while the others settled down to enjoy the tea Adela poured out, seeming aware that Claudia had a spot of difficulty at the moment.

"You look dazed. Is something wrong?" He offered her a cup of tea that she took with a not-too-steady hand.

How could he sound so concerned, almost tender in his regard? He was a fraud! "I am quite all right, my lord," she replied in a stiff voice. She took refuge in a sip of tea.

He glanced at the list she had begun to make with the intention of sending an order to Madame Clotilde in London.

"Green velvet? Good. But it should be a soft bluish-green, not harsh, I believe. The blue sarsenet ought to have a hint of violet in it to set off your skin and hair. And almond pink kerseymere? Too insipid, my dear. Perhaps a wild rose might do."

"I should bow to your obviously great experience in selecting women's garments, my lord," Claudia said with a touch of acid in her voice. "It would seem you are most gifted at it. Does that stem from considerable experience or merely observation?" Claudia moved a piece of paper to cover her list. Not allowing him the satisfaction of knowing whether she truly intended to order as he suggested, she rose to join the others at the table where Adela had poured out tea. Holding her saucer and cup in hand, she surveyed Adela.

"How sweet you are, dear friend, to pour tea for thirsty callers whilst I am otherwise occupied." She slid onto the sofa and exchanged a speaking look with Adela. Then Claudia poured tea for Lord Hawke, offering him the plate of dainties as well.

Lastly she again took refuge in her cup of tea. The steaming brew was precisely what she needed to restore her wits.

The vicar, deprived of his admirer and wary of the London gentlemen, departed after issuing a gentle warning to Edward not to overdo and by all means to leave his war toys alone.

When the front door closed behind him Hawke murmured, "Prosy boor. How dare he tell Edward how to go on when we are all here to care for the lad?"

"How indeed?" Claudia replied, for once in perfect agreement with Lord Hawke.

Tea consumed, the gentlemen—minus Lord Hawke and Claudia—took their ladies out to the terrace along with Edward and the fine boat. Within moments Claudia could hear his delighted squeals with loud encouragement from the various men.

"It seems that Edward enjoys your gift. Thank you for being so thoughtful of him." She knew she sounded less than gracious, but the boat on top of realizing that she had tumbled into love with her dratted coguardian was simply too much to stomach.

"On that order . . . If you like I could take it to London with me. Madame Clotilde is quite gifted, as my aunt has remarked time and again. She will know which fabric is best."

Claudia gave him a startled look. "You are going to London?" It was a stupid question. If he said he was going away, he certainly was.

"A quick trip for a minor requirement. Nothing serious, I assure you." He walked closer to where she now stood. With a deftness she could only be in awe of, he filched the list from under the other paper and tucked it in his pocket. His smile seemed predatory. "Allow me to assist, my dear."

Claudia took a step back—never mind that she wished she could be in his arms. *That* was stupid. Her little desk was in the path of her retreat. Swallowing with care she nodded. "I am glad it is nothing serious. But you need not take that list. Indeed, I may add another gown, or perhaps change my mind."

"They will do for a beginning." One hand reached out to touch her hair. He flipped off the dainty day cap she always wore. "There. You are not so old that you need resort to a cap. And you are definitely not a spinster, nor, may I add, do you kiss like one." His gaze was challenging.

Claudia wildly considered dashing out of the room. The only trouble with that notion is that her feet refused to obey her.

"Nothing to say? Good." He stepped closer until there was no daylight between them. Then that audacious hand trailed down her jaw until reaching her chin.

She simply could not move. The look in those amazingly blue eyes held her still as though she were bound in place.

And then his lips touched hers. Miraculously, fire did not scorch her, nor did she faint dead away. Rather, she foolishly leaned into his kiss, accepting it. Nay, her lips pleaded with his never to stop his assault. Her hands, rather than push him away, crept up the front of that well-tailored navy coat to touch the back of his crisp, dark hair. This might be as close to heaven as she would be allowed.

He gathered her tightly in his arms. And proceeded to kiss her quite thoroughly in ways she had never experienced before. A quick learner, she participated fully, relishing the intimate contact. *After all,* a wee voice in the back of her head said, *you might as well take what you are offered. It may never come your way again!*

At last he withdrew just enough to survey her face.

Oh, how she longed to wipe that smug expression from his face. She wouldn't dignify the kiss with a show of outrage, however. *That* was something for a virginal miss, which she most assuredly was not! Like everything else he did, he kissed exceedingly well. The wicked thought slipped into her mind, a wondering how Lord Hawke would be at his husbandly duty. And that naughty notion brought a blush to her cheeks.

Hawke gazed down at the adorably confused woman before him. He had kissed many women, but never one who affected him as Claudia, Lady Fairfax did. He cleared his throat, wondering when would be the proper time to speak to her about her future.

"Look, Mama! Come and see!" Edward's piping voice commanded. "The boat is wonderful."

Hawke smiled. The boat wasn't the only thing that was wonderful around here. "Shall we join the others, my dear?"

She nodded. As they walked toward the terrace she spoke at last, softly and with deliberation. "I am not your dear, you know. And if you truly want that strip of land, talk to Fry. He can tell you what it is worth."

She hurried ahead of him, leaving Hawke stunned. He kissed her until they were both nearly senseless, and she had the temerity to speak of land? What had brought that into her head?

He followed Claudia to the curving stone wall with the channel running along the top of it. Edward demonstrated just how well the boat would sail, demanding that Hawke admire the trim lines and the way it could go.

"I think that if I could put it in the stream it would be smashingly fast," the boy said. He leaned toward Hawke in a confiding way, adding, "I don't suppose Mama will let me near the stream until this bandage comes off. But you could test the boat for me, couldn't you? I might even be able to watch?"

Not proof against a pair of wide brown eyes so full of hope, Hawke nodded. "Perhaps later on. I leave

for London in the morning." When Edward's counte-
nance fell, Hawke added, "I won't be gone long. Probably be back before you have time to miss me. And
besides, Elliot, Pace, and Lodge will remain here.
They will continue to help you with the battle scene."
Hawke resolved to find something to add to the splen-
dor of the Spanish mountain landscape.

Edward looked to the other gentlemen who were
chatting with the three women. "Cousin Olivia looks
pretty today," he observed. "Miss Cork always looks
nice. So does Lady Dunston. But my mama is best of
all," he concluded smugly.

"I will agree with you there, my lad," Hawke said
quietly.

It was coming on to dinnertime when the gentlemen
reluctantly departed. Claudia knew that Olivia, Dorothy, and Adela would have been delighted if the men
had been invited to remain for dinner. Claudia knew
her nerves simply wouldn't tolerate it. Frazzled didn't
begin to cover her condition.

She left the women to discuss the afternoon and
sought out Mr. Fry. When she found him in the muniment room she smiled at him. "Mr. Fry, Lord Hawke
desires to purchase that strip of land that was once
part of his estate. Could you come up with a fair price
on the property, and send it over to Mr. Logan?"

He gave her an astounded look, but nodded his
agreement to do as she wished. "I hadn't thought you
would sell, ma'am."

"Well, I shall. Also, would you arrange for the interior
of the dower house to be painted? I think a soft yellow
drab for the drawing room and perhaps that nice red
for the dining room—you know the one I mean?"

"The one called 'better class red'? Indeed, my lady."
He jotted the colors down on a pad at his elbow.

"I think pale verdigris for the smaller bedroom and
perhaps the yellow drab for the larger bedroom—the
halls as well. That little back bedroom could be papered

in a pretty blue flower print." She gave him an uncertain look. "Perhaps the kitchen could do with a coat of pale ochre?" It was spur of the moment. She needed another pursuit, one that would occupy her mind.

"I will obtain a book on papers, my lady. The dower house has been neglected for far too long. It is an excellent thing that you repair the house before it becomes truly sorry." His expression of approval was nearly her undoing.

Claudia mumbled a vague reply, then drifted back to the central hall. Why she bothered with the painting she didn't know, but as Fry said, the place had been badly neglected. Even if she bought a house, the dower house should be in order. Edward could rent it out. The more she thought about it, the more she realized that she would have to move a greater distance from here than to Tunbridge Wells. Bath might be just the place.

And painting the dower house would certainly give Lord Hawke a pause. That and the paper from Fry on the price for that strip of land!

"You seem pleased with yourself," Adela said with a saucy look at Claudia. "What have you been up to, dear girl?"

"I instructed Fry to send Mr. Logan the fair price for that land Lord Hawke wants to own. And I also ordered the dower house to be painted."

"The dower house?" Olivia cried in surprise. "But you will not require the use of that for many years."

"Fry says it is in bad need of repair. I suspect some water damage. The roof must be gone over as well. I suppose I might rent it out." She glanced at Adela, then took her place at her desk again. It was then she recalled that Lord Hawke had filched her dress list when she was still reeling from that momentous kiss. "That miserable creature!" she said with feeling.

"Now what has happened?" Adela inquired, cross-

ing the Turkey carpet to stand by the desk, giving
Claudia a warmly sympathetic look.

"That man took my list." Claudia sniffed in derision.

Adela made no pretense as to what list Claudia was
talking about. "Good grief! What would he want with it?"

"He travels to London on the morrow and said he
would personally deliver it to Madame Clotilde. I
might have changed my mind about the colors. And I
had written nothing about the styles I wanted! Oh, he
is the most vexing creature alive!"

"Vexing, perhaps, but oh, my dear, he is handsome," Adela purred, her eyes assuming a somewhat
dreamy look. "If I know Lord Hawke at all, he will
describe you to Madame and tell her to do her very
best with those colors and the latest styles."

"Good heavens. You truly think that he might do
such a thing?" Claudia asked, her cheeks warming
with a blush.

"I chanced to pause at the doorway from the terrace
while you and the viscount were so well occupied. He
will do exceedingly well."

Claudia, quite unable to stand up to the teasing look
in Adela's eyes, rose from her chair. Walking over to
where Olivia and Dorothy sat idly paging through the various lady's magazines that had been stacked on the table,
she said, "I expect dinner will be ready before long.
Shall we dress? Or shall we simply remain as we are?"

Adela chuckled. "I believe we are all longing to
relax and be ourselves after an afternoon of entertaining gentlemen. I vote that we not bother to change."

The others agreed. "Dorothy did not bring a vast
assortment of garments along. And I am more than
content as I am," Olivia confided, shyly smiling. Her
interest in Mr. Lodge had turned her into a very
pretty woman.

Claudia said nothing. She was beyond words at
this point.

Chapter Fourteen

Without the threat of Lord Hawke popping up when least wanted, Claudia was able to relax the next morning. She shunted her feelings for him to the back of her mind. Her reaction to him when she saw the dratted man, her foolish quivering when she found those intensely blue eyes fixed on her, her desire for his touch—all were banished from thought. Or, at least she tried to do that. At times, these things would sneak into her mind and she would discover Lord Hawke had taken residence in her thoughts, no matter how she tried to keep him at bay.

She rose quite early, looked in on Edward, and then—seeing that her guests were still abed—went to the small room she used as a painting studio that was adjacent to the muniment room.

The design for Edward's dragon took time to transfer to the plain white ceramic plate. She worked carefully until satisfied with the end result. She would paint it later, then fire it.

The kiln she used was not the best design. She contemplated having a new one constructed. There certainly was sufficient room on the property to have one some distance from the house. She had the present one between the dairy and the laundry. It was a tolerable arrangement, considering how seldom she had used the kiln of late. If she continued with her plans to paint a set of dishes with the flowers and fairies she envisioned, she would like a newer and better kiln.

Claudia stepped into the next room where Mr. Fry was at work, thinking she might suggest a new kiln to him and see what he had to say about it.

He looked up from the stack of papers he had assembled for the transfer of property. She saw a deed and other legal-looking sheets. "I have just completed the estimate on the value of that parcel of land, my lady. I intend to meet with Logan today if that is agreeable with you." He handed her a long sheet of paper that had the whereas and wherewith clauses containing his suggested value. "If this meets with his lordship's approval the transaction should take no time at all. May I inquire if you have a specific project in mind for the money?" Had he not been an old and trusted employee, that question would have been totally out of bounds. "What I mean to say is, if there is any manner in which I might assist you, you have only to ask."

Claudia knew he must have speculated on her sale of her property. It was not surprising that he should. That didn't mean she would reveal her intentions, however. Women were supposedly not capable of handling their own estates. Men tended to believe that because their heads were smaller in size that their brains were also smaller, hence unable to think well. When Claudia considered the number of women who managed the family estates while husbands were either off in London or at sea, she could not help but laugh at that silly notion. She had exchanged letters with a few of these women, seeking counsel on how they coped. It had been an illuminating and instructional experience.

"I thought it time that the property revert to the original owner," she hedged. "I understand that Lord Hawke has attempted to purchase that parcel in the past."

"True," Mr. Fry agreed. "At that time you were not interested in dealing with his lordship."

"Once I have the money in hand, there is an investment I may consider." That was sufficiently vague, but it allowed Mr. Fry to understand that she did have something specific in mind. She quite ignored the bit about refusing to deal with Lord Hawke in the past. She'd had her reasons, and she was not about to reveal them. "Mr. Fry, I would like to have a new kiln built. Would you be so kind as to find out particulars for me? I am not satisfied with the present one."

"Indeed, my lady. I will look into the matter at once." If he entertained any opinion on her painting or the fairies or anything else she fancied he kept that to himself.

He gathered the papers pertaining to the property sale and tucked them into a case before giving Claudia a hesitant look. "I shall deliver these to Logan immediately."

She nodded. "Lord Hawke has gone to London. I expect he will handle whatever is necessary when he returns."

Returning to her painting room, she began the delicate task of coloring the dragon. She worked for a brief time, laying in the ground for the dragon. A glance at the wall clock told her that it was past time she joined her guests. It was far too easy to forget about time when involved in her painting.

She found the women assembled in the breakfast room. From the half-full cups and crumbs on the various plates, she was tardy in her appearance. She apologized at once.

"When I am painting, the time tends to slip past me and before I know it, an hour has gone by."

Adela wore a strangely anticipatory expression on her face. It was as though she knew something and wasn't certain how Claudia would accept it. She had something to share, and judging by her expression she was of mixed feelings about its reception.

Claudia poured herself a cup of tea, taking it along with a still warm scone to the table. She waited for Adela to speak.

"It has been a lovely visit," Adela began. "I have truly enjoyed myself so much."

"But?" Claudia asked, thinking she knew what was to follow.

"I am returning to London. If you like, I can bring any additional instructions to Madame Clotilde for you." She gave Claudia a hopeful smile.

"Perhaps one or two," Claudia replied pensively. "I am sorry to see you leave. I have enjoyed your visit."

Adela toyed with her spoon, clinking it about in her teacup. "Lord Elliot will travel with me." Dead silence followed this casually dropped bomb.

"Oh?" Claudia approached the subject with care. She was not about to wish her dear friend a happy marriage if it was to be something else altogether.

"To put your mind at ease, we plan to be married and soon." Adela's smile grew radiant. "Max will get a license in London so we will not need the banns read. At my age and being a widow, I far prefer the privacy."

"I am so pleased the two of you will be married," Olivia cried in delight. "I cannot imagine two people better suited to one another." She glanced at Claudia and Dorothy Cox and blushed. "Of course, there are other ideal couples. It is just that you are, that is . . ." she floundered.

"I am pleased as well, Adela," Claudia added. "How grand I feel, to think I have helped bring you two together. I expect Lord Hawke will be quite amazed at the coming marriage."

"As to that, I am certain ours will not be the only pairing from this auspicious stay in the country. Surely you, Miss Greene, are quite enamored of Mr. Lodge. And I believe he returns your regard in full. I have observed his gaze rest on you with more than tender esteem." Adela's eyes gleamed as she gently teased Olivia.

Olivia made no reply. Claudia gathered she was beyond speech, pink with embarrassment and probably pleasure. The vicar had assuredly been given his congé, whether he knew it or not.

Adela turned to Dorothy Cox. "And you, Miss Cox. I have seen the way Lord Pace looks at you. I'd not be surprised were a wedding to come about for you two. You have such similar interests." Adela sipped her tea, watching the younger woman.

Dorothy smiled. "I have a high respect for Lord Pace. Do you know that he is acquainted with my cousin, Sir Ralph Newby? Sir Ralph wrote my father a letter in which he praised Lord Pace highly— especially his horses! We shall see what comes, but regardless, I shall always be in Lady Fairfax's debt for allowing me this splendid experience."

Claudia knew her smile was a trifle forced. "I am delighted my spur-of-the-moment gathering has come off so well. Miss Cox, you need not return home unless you wish. We have had such a pleasant time with you here. Olivia and I rattle around in this large house. I have enjoyed having others about."

Olivia found her tongue. "Oh, yes, indeed, it is so. I truly welcome your company. Yours as well, Lady Dunston."

Nothing was said about any possible development between Claudia and Lord Hawke, even though he had come to Fairfax Hall daily before he went to London. His guardianship might be an excuse for something more significant. No one would chance any speculation on it.

"Well, I had best attend to my departure. My footman and coachman have the carriage ready. My maid will have my things packed by now. I was merely waiting for you," she said to Claudia, "to offer my news and farewell."

"You said Lord Elliot will ride with you?" Claudia hoped that the dashing Adela would not flout convention too much.

"It will be a nicely crowded carriage with my maid and his valet inside. Max will tie his horse on behind for at least part of the trip. Simon will ride on the bench with the coachman. All is in readiness." She rose from the table, shook hands with Dorothy Cox and Olivia, then bestowed an affectionate hug and kiss on her dearest friend. "I will write you all the details."

"See that you do," Claudia insisted. "I shall await the news of the wedding. Mind you, I want details—your gown, the flowers, who attends you. I am sorry I cannot join you for the happy occasion. I imagine Lord Hawke will be there."

Adela looked amused. "Perhaps. Lord Elliot and I wish for the wedding to be very quiet. We shall disappoint everyone and probably have my maid and his valet attend us."

She left the breakfast room amid cries of dismay.

Once the entourage had departed and the house had fallen into the familiar quiet, the remaining three women met over a light luncheon.

Claudia eyed Olivia and Dorothy. "Mr. Lodge and Lord Pace will more than likely be over shortly. Do have the horses saddled and go for a ride if you wish. This fine weather will not last forever." Claudia did not want to go along with them, thinking it would spoil the progress of the two alliances. "I intend to paint this afternoon, so you would not see me regardless."

The other two exchanged looks, and beamed a smile at Claudia, causing her to think they had worried about her being alone while they went off with their beaux. She wished them well. Just because her life was all confusion didn't mean she could not want happiness for her friends.

Thus when the gentlemen arrived, they found Olivia and Dorothy dressed in their habits and their mounts saddled and waiting. The men were obviously delighted that they wouldn't have to wait around while the women changed.

From the sitting room window Claudia watched them go, headed in much the same direction as the previous ride when the entire party had taken off with Edward and his new pony. And Lord Hawke. When they were lost to her view, she wandered along to her painting room.

A patter of feet in the hall behind her brought her around to see who followed her. She smiled and extended a hand to her stepson. "Edward, are you having a good day?"

"May I see my dragon, Mama?" Edward asked politely. He had his grand new boat in hand, seeming ready to try the stone channel again.

"I am in the process of painting it. Come, I will show you what has been done so far." Hand in hand they went to her painting room where Edward expressed satisfaction at his very own dragon—albeit on a plate.

In London, Hawke smiled with satisfaction. He had paid a call on Madame Clotilde with the result that Claudia's order had been handed in—along with his own and quite separate instructions. He did the incredible thing of paying for his purchases in advance. He knew that in doing so his order would receive immediate attention. Madame had the directions for shipping both orders when finished. She also had Lady Fairfax's measurements; that was all she required now that she had payment! She raised no eyebrows. Madame Clotilde had not reached the pinnacle of her profession by being indiscreet.

The other tasks he had set himself were accomplished with dispatch. With great pleasure he was able to bid his London staff a temporary good-bye before heading to Hawke's Rest. This time he relaxed in his crested carriage, not to impress, but so it would be available when needed. Nothing would be too fine for what he had in mind.

He had done a bit of investigation into Claudia's family and admitted to being impressed with her relatives. Her sisters had certainly married well. In particular he had noted the eminently powerful earl, Lord Stanwell. Claudia could claim some prestige as far as her position in society was concerned.

It made no difference to his plans. He had laid them with care. The only matter that gave him pause—well, two matters actually—were her childlessness and this rubbish about seeing fairies. Surely the latter was absurd. The first was of greater import. It would require a considerable amount of deliberation. He had to admit that with a woman who had not been married whether or not she might bear a child was an unknown factor. The lack of children might have been Lord Fairfax's fault. She came from a large family, so perhaps she merely needed the right partner. Fairfax had likely spent too much time with Mrs. Norton.

It was only by chance that he happened to stop over at the same inn where Lord Elliot and Lady Dunston also paused in their journey to London.

"I must say this is a surprise." With a grin, Hawke surveyed two rather self-conscious faces. "You needn't say a word. I can be as blind as the next fellow if desired."

"Hawke, you are detestable. I'll have you know that Elliot and I are to be married once we reach London." Lady Dunston gave him an amused look before turning an adoring gaze on Elliot.

"In that event, I wish you both the very best." Hawke paused a moment, then added, "Lodge and Pace stayed on?"

"You said you would only be a few days and so you are. Besides, they both have interests that lure them into remaining at Hawke's Rest." Elliot exchanged a knowing look with Hawke.

"If you mean Miss Greene and Miss Cork, you could as well say so," Lady Dunston said with a sniff. "I trust they will not be slow tops and will give those darling girls assurances of a happily married future."

"One can only hope," Elliot added, a gleam in his eyes.

Hawke pleaded hunger and fatigue and spoke of an early bed, insisting he wanted to get away as early as possible in the morning. He had no wish to be a burden on the loving couple with his company. Their warm looks could have lit the fire in the hearth.

Hawke wondered what it would be like to receive such a look from Claudia Fairfax. The few occasions when he had held her in his arms had been most illuminating. She had progressed from untutored response to eager participation. What lay beyond that he happily contemplated while he sought sleep. The nagging bit about her childlessness he tucked away to be mulled over some moment in the future.

The first thing he confronted when he entered his home the next morning was the information that Logan wished to see him immediately.

"What is so important that I must seek you out at once?" Hawke inquired in a deceptively lazy manner as he entered his steward's office.

Logan, well acquainted with his lordship's conduct, merely handed him the sheaf of papers brought over by Mr. Fry.

"An offer to sell? Any idea what changed her mind? She refused the last offer I made—or rather Fry said he thought it impossible. What sort of maggot has she got in her head now?"

"Fry hinted she has some investment in mind. What it might be is more than I could guess." Logan watched as his lordship studied the paper, then signed where necessary.

"There. A matter that has troubled our family for years is at last settled. See that a draft for the sum is transferred to Lady Fairfax at once." When Logan raised his brows in question, Hawke added, "Women are known to change their minds. I don't want Lady Fairfax to have second thoughts."

Logan laughed and gathered the papers together before finding the required bank draft for Lord Hawke to sign. When that was accomplished Hawke moved toward the door.

"I assume this is a matter of haste so I will go to the Hall at once," Logan said, placing the papers in a case. "I am sure Fry expects me once he knows you are to home."

Hawke nodded and strolled along the corridor leading back to the central hall where he found his butler supervising the disposition of his belongings that had come from London. Hawke smiled at the look of satisfaction on Slade's face at the number of cases and parcels carried into the house.

"It seems as though you intend to be here for a time, my lord," Slade said when he became aware his employer stood to one side of the hall watching him.

"I'll have to see how things go. Are Lord Pace and Mr. Lodge anywhere about?" Other than the footmen bustling about with the luggage and parcels the house was quiet.

"I believe they rode over to Fairfax Hall with the intention of a leisurely ride with Miss Greene and Miss Cork." Slade exchanged an eloquent look with his employer.

"So it is as I hoped. And Lady Fairfax? She remains at the Hall?" Hawke was casual in his questioning but with Lady Dunston gone, he wished to know what was afoot next door. If anyone would know it would be Slade.

"It is my understanding, sir." The butler raised a brow at the footman who waited with a parcel. The lad hurried up the stairs to Lord Hawke's bedroom with his burden.

Hawke took his time to change his clothes and make certain he looked his best before leaving the house for Fairfax Hall. When he arrived there, James, the young footman he had assigned to duty at the hall, opened the door to him.

"All is well here, I trust?" he inquired casually.

"Indeed, my lord. Lady Fairfax is a kind and generous employer." The earnestly spoken words brought a raised brow from Hawke, nothing more.

"I should like to see Lady Fairfax. Is she about?"

James glanced at the tall longcase clock, then back to Hawke. "I believe she is in her painting room."

"I should like to see this place," Hawke said. "Never mind showing me the way. I know the layout of this house as well as my own."

Striding along the corridor to the rear of the house where the various offices were located, Hawke observed how clean and well organized everything was. If she painted fairies and dragons, she was also an excellent manager of her household. Even with the best housekeeper employed, a well-run home required a mistress who knew what was required.

He passed the muniment room, not stopping to have words with Fry and Logan. Those gentlemen didn't so much as glance up from the papers in which they were immersed.

Upon reaching the "painting" room, he paused at the door. Claudia wore that idiotic white lace cap on her glorious golden hair. The first thing he wanted to do was bury it somewhere that she couldn't find it. All the other caps he would hide as well.

Although he said not a word, something must have alerted her that she was being observed. She looked up from the plate she'd been painting. Her unguarded expression was quite a revelation—one he appreciated fully.

"Good afternoon. I thought you were in London." She placed her paintbrush on the table with care.

"As you see, I am home again."

"I am flattered you sought me out so soon," she said, a sly smile lighting her eyes. "Is there a problem with the sale you wished to discuss? Fry said he thought the price offered for the parcel of land is fair."

"More than fair. I sent over the draft on my bank for the full amount." He slowly moved into the room to where she sat. "I wish to see what you paint." Looking around the room, he noted several nicely painted plates on wall racks. "You did these, of course." There was little doubt of that, for the designs depicted lush roses and other garden flowers with shy, very tiny, fairies peeping around the blooms. To his amazement, he found them rather endearing.

Claudia sat before the dragon plate, watching him, most likely gauging his reaction to her work.

"You are an astonishing artist. I have never seen anything like these. The flowers are beautifully done; the fairies are delightful. And you intend to do an entire set of dishes similar to these?"

"Indeed," she said on an exhale of breath, as though she had been holding it while he looked at her plates. "I should like to accomplish just that. The china I ordered from the Royal Worcester factory is stacked over there." She gestured to one side. "It is nice of them to offer blank china for a person to decorate as she pleases."

"Hmm." He turned to study the plate she now painted. It was Edward's dragon. Hawke grinned at the whimsical creature peering up from the plate. "Reminds me of the newts on my garden wall."

Claudia chuckled. "Well, as to that, I confess I did study one I found on that new wall constructed for Edward's pleasure. I wonder if the concept of a dragon didn't develop from a creature perhaps larger than our little English newt?"

Her chuckle and candor at the model she'd used for the dragon captivated Hawke. "A touch of the Chinese and you have Edward's splendid dragon." He paused for a moment before continuing. "What made you decide to sell the land?"

She evaded his gaze, looking down at her plate instead.

"Logan said you had an investment in mind," he prompted.

"It is merely a germ of a notion. I thought it would be nice to have a small house in Bath. Many widows settle there. Eventually Edward will not require my presence. Although I have ordered the dower house painted inside and out, it is more for preservation than for my living there. I think Edward deserves to be on his own—in time."

He assumed a thoughtful look, then nodded. "I believe that would be a wise investment, my dear. You continually surprise me with your astuteness. Bath is bound to remain a charming place, one that will draw people over time."

She looked astonished at his words and he couldn't help but smile. "I doubt you will actually live there. However, it would be a pleasant place to visit."

With that he changed the topic to her obvious frustration. Time was on his side, and he intended to make full use of every minute he had.

"Now explain what you plan with the china. How many place settings, and will they be for dinner or luncheon, and do you intend to do serving pieces as well?"

She blinked several times, then answered him in a somewhat bewildered manner.

Hawke nodded sagely to her reply, revealing nothing of his thoughts.

Chapter Fifteen

*C*laudia sat quietly while she tried to assimilate what had just happened. Lord Hawke had sauntered into her painting room and charmed her into talking far too much about her life and plans. Had she really told him of her intention to buy a house in Bath? And had he actually said it might be a good idea, but that she wouldn't live there? Did the man think to insist she remain at the dower house forever? Merely because he was Edward's guardian did not mean he was hers as well!

"It is a lovely day—far too nice to remain in the house." He shot her a look that promised a scheme. "You will have ample opportunity to paint when the weather becomes inclement. Come," he persuaded with that slow smile she didn't quite trust, "let's go for a ride."

"Edward longs to have his dragon plate," she countered, unwilling to be in even remotely intimate association with him. The last time they had gone riding it had culminated in that kiss that had shaken her to her toes.

"My head gardener tells me it will rain tomorrow. You can paint then." He covered her paints with the cloth she used, then took her brush, dipped it in the cleaner and carefully wiped it.

"You leave me little choice, my lord." She flashed

him an annoyed look. And where had he learned about the necessity of properly cleaning a brush? The man thought he could ride roughshod over her plans. The problem was . . . he could. She hated the way she gave in to him, but he could be so beguiling. And she had to admit that she enjoyed being with him, even if he confused her and unsettled her from top to toe . . . if he kissed her, that is. She wondered what his intent might be this time. The fascinating image that brought forth urged her to accept.

"You could at least call me Hawke," he complained with that charming smile remaining to tease her.

"Very well, Hawke, for it suits you to a cow's thumb." She took a calming breath and slipped from her stool. He stopped her at the doorway, staring at her with a most disconcerting gaze.

"You think of me as a hawk? A creature of prey?" He studied her. She didn't know what was in his mind but whatever it might be, it lit those intensely blue eyes like a candle flame.

"What else?" She slipped past him to march up to her room where she changed into her blue habit for the ride.

Once dressed she checked her appearance in the looking glass before turning to her maid. "Mary, tell Edward he may come with us for a ride on his pony."

"But my lady, the boy oughtn't be on his pony with that great bandage on his arm," the maid reminded. "If he was to injure it again, it might never heal right."

The maid was correct. It was a prime example of how Hawke befuddled her brains. Claudia would never forgive herself if Edward's arm did not heal properly. "Botheration," she muttered as she went to look in on her stepson. An inspection of his stiffened bandage convinced her that she would have to go it alone with Hawke. She'd not ask Olivia to join them for it would be an admission of sorts—an admission that Claudia dare not be alone with Hawke. Naturally this was true, but she hated to give him that power over her. Perhaps she might suggest a groom for the sake of propriety?

As she marched down the stairs she wondered what excuse Hawke would invent to make a groom unnecessary.

Hawke joined her at the bottom of the stairs, walking with her to the stable where the horse Hawke had lent her was still stabled. The two horses were saddled and awaiting them. Jem Groom was in the stables grooming Edward's pony Humbug. She was aware he watched her with Hawke.

The gentle chestnut greeted a somewhat wary Claudia with a soft nicker. Kismet snorted as though in scorn. Claudia made her way to the mounting block and prepared to mount her horse, wishing she might ride astride. It looked to be far easier than coping with the sidesaddle. But then, her skirts would rise and she would truly be scandalous! Hawke would probably enjoy the sight of her revealed ankles. He seemed the sort.

Hawke ignored the mounting block and easily lifted Claudia to her saddle.

She truly tried to ignore the sensations ignited by his firm touch at her waist. Even through the soft navy kerseymere of her habit she was far too aware of his hands.

"I thought perhaps we should have Jem Groom ride with us. Respectability, you know. It would not do for some gossip to claim impropriety." If she sounded a bit breathless surely he might account it to her hurried change? "You never know when you may encounter someone else while out riding."

"You feel you must be so circumspect? I doubt anyone would say a word, for it is well known that I am Edward's coguardian. There is nothing unseemly in our riding out together. Besides, we will be on our land. Who could object?"

Hawke sounded so matter of fact that he soothed her fears. She was being childishly skittish. Squaring her shoulders, she urged her inner self to be firm, to resist this man who had the power to reduce her to quivering jelly. Mastering her inner qualms, she perched atop Folly thinking that she and the horse could have the same name, for surely it was a folly for her to be so complacent.

They covered much the same territory they had on that previous ride. Only this time they were alone. Jem Groom had agreed to walk Edward around on a lead, a gentle pace and certainly done with extreme care. The boy had entered the stable just before Claudia rode out with Hawke. He hadn't minded being left behind in the least. When Jem said Edward needed more practice, Edward took it as gospel.

The pair of riders maintained silence for a time. Claudia wondered how she might break it, examining and discarding several topics as she rode. It was Hawke who intruded on the bucolic peace.

"You paint very well, my dear. Do you have the designs for the fairy plates worked out as yet?" He spoke in a casual manner. There was no sign of censure in his voice, nothing to say he thought her fairies a pack of nonsense.

She gave him a curious look. If he didn't tease her, what was in the back of his mind? "I have a number of sketches that I have done over the past spring and summer. I must polish them before attempting to transfer the drawings to the porcelain. I would like to find a fine example of small blue scabious and red clover as an example of late summer blooms. Then there are autumn flowers to sketch as well. China asters and mums, you know. Michaelmas daisies as well."

"There is a patch of red clover on one of my fields. Come, I will show you where to find it." With an engaging grin, he led her off the path and down into a meadow.

Pleased to see he was not teasing her, or simply attempting to get her alone for another kiss, Claudia beamed him a smile of delight when they reached the patch of colorful wildflowers. "Help me down, please. I want to gather a few to take back for study." Within minutes she was on the ground and kneeling by the red clover patch. "These are prime examples." She picked a handful of blooms along with leaves. "Of course this means I must return to the Hall at once."

Her smile was crafty. She knew he wanted to remain out, away from others, for a time. She wasn't certain why, but his snatching a kiss did occur to her.

"But you have not shown me any fairies. I insist on that."

Claudia had no desire to walk all the way back to the Hall nor could she mount Folly without his help, and he seemed distinctly reluctant to offer that. She considered what pretext she might give to wiggle out of this predicament.

"I doubt they will come out for you." She decided he had to accept that excuse. Surely he didn't think she could command the fairies to appear at her wish?

"I suppose you must see them at dawn or sunset? Or must you sing to them to lure them forth?" Hawke said in that rich voice that slightly reminded her of treacle. She adored treacle pudding, and she very much feared she was coming to adore this man as well. What would he say if he knew how her foolish heart behaved? Treacle pudding was a nursery treat. Was he her treat? The image that brought forth surely put a blush on her cheeks. She could feel it creep over her skin. Blondes were so fair of skin that she knew it could be seen. Mercifully, he said nothing. But she had little doubt he had noticed it. Those eyes of his never missed a thing, or so it seemed.

He placed a hand at her elbow, causing those silly moths in her tummy to begin a wild performance of the Lancers. Again. Really, she must discipline herself better. But that was all well and good to *think*. The rest of her refused to obey. She was nothing more than a bunch of nerves.

"Dawn is a fine time," she replied.

"I will be over early one of these days so you may show me your fairies."

He stepped closer to her and she found it impossible to retreat. A shrub stood precisely in her way. Besides, did she truly wish to retreat? Honesty compelled her to admit to herself that she would not be averse to another of his salutes. The previous ones had been so enlightening. "Very well," she managed to say— whether to his request or what she wished to be she could not have said.

Quite as though he read her mind, he reached out to bring her closer to him, right up against that splendid riding coat. Of course there were too many layers of clothing for her to feel scorched as she had in the garden. Still, his body pressed against hers was disturbing. It brought her senses to life—what few senses that had not already sprung into being.

His kiss began gently, as though he did not wish to frighten her. As if he could shock her this time! She had unconsciously been longing for his touch since the last kiss. However, she found the visions that inveigled their way into her mind very disturbing. She had been married, after all. She knew full well what ought to follow such tempting, delicious kisses.

He deepened the kiss. It was quite as though each time they kissed he drew her deeper into a more intense relationship.

Somehow she found the strength to pull away from him. How, she couldn't imagine, but she did. After running the tip of her tongue over her lips, she said,

"I imagine we had best return now. The flowers will wilt."

Hawke's lazy grin almost did her in. Actually, it almost drew her back into his arms again. Never had she confronted a more beguiling face, a more tempting fate. She knew without a doubt that he wanted her.

She turned aside, walking quickly to Folly. "Help me, will you, Hawke?" He might want her. He couldn't have her. She would cling to her respectability at all costs, no matter what that little voice in the back of her brain told her. And now it almost whined, reminding her of what she undoubtedly missed, what all had been neglected during her married life. It was vastly unfair that life should be so cruel!

The following days were full. Hawke seemed to be underfoot more often than not. Claudia wondered if he did not have something requiring his attention at Hawke's Rest, but he blandly insisted that all was well at his estate. He conferred with Fry on the draining of the bottomland, and discussed the matter of the sheep breeding improvements. At first Claudia thought he was going over her head to countermand her orders. But rather, he listened to what Fry said and appeared to approve her plans. How shocking!

She was far too aware of him, no matter where he went or what he did. Perhaps she was developing a special sense that applied only to him?

A week later he brought over the little carved buildings to go with the set of soldiers Adela had given Edward. He claimed Claudia had to assist in placing them on the table set aside just for Edward's battle scene. He guided her with a light touch on her shoulder, a touch she felt all the way to her toes.

All he had to do was look at her and she seemed to sense his regard. Why! That matter plagued her into the dim hours of the night. What was his purpose in all this? He had ridden into London to manage some business—why could he not have remained there for a time?

She left Hawke with Edward in the room where the soldiers and an elaborate scene had been staged. They were deep in a discussion of strategy, Hawke offering simple suggestions and explanations, when she slipped away. Within moments she wished she had remained. As she reached the bottom of the stairs, James ushered in the vicar.

"Vicar Woodley. What a surprise." She gestured to the drawing room, the formal chill of that area quite suited her mood of the moment. "Inform Mrs. Tibbins I wish tea in the drawing room, please," she added to James.

The vicar looked about him with an assessing gaze, quite as though he intended to purchase the house. Encroaching man!

James disappeared down the hall, intent upon obeying the command given him. There was a wager belowstairs that had to do with whether or not Viscount Hawke would succeed in, one—getting Edward off to Eton, and two—getting married to Lady Fairfax. James had placed his bet that Hawke would succeed on both counts. He knew his employer well enough to know that he was rarely defeated. It was in the footman's interest to see to it that the vicar was thwarted in his unctuous intentions, whatever they might be!

"To what do I owe the pleasure of your call, Vicar Woodley?" Claudia was chillingly polite, showing him to a side chair while selecting a nearby one for herself. Sitting as stiffly as she could, she fixed an inquiring gaze on the man. He seemed ill at ease. Perhaps she was too off-putting? She devoutly hoped so.

"My dear Lady Fairfax, surely you know what great esteem I have for you? I have enjoyed my many calls to this house to tutor Edward and to partake of an occasional meal at your bountiful table. My request should not come as a surprise. Nay, I flatter myself that you must have expected it for some time."

Before he could continue, Mrs. Tibbins bustled in with a large tray that held not only all that was needed for tea, but a plate of the vicar's favorite scones. The housekeeper lingered until James took his position beside the table.

At once Claudia began the ritual of serving tea, inquiring as to whether he wished milk or lemon, quite as though she had totally forgotten his preferences. She hoped this might discourage him. She dispensed the tea, with the help of the suddenly fussy James, who appeared to take pleasure in passing the scones, inquiring about the desirability of more tea, and in general making a nuisance of himself. Claudia made a mental note to give him a raise.

At last the scones were gone, every crumb. The teapot was dry. And she had no excuse for not permitting the vicar to speak.

"And now, what could I possibly expect, sir? Do you come to tell me that you think it time for Edward to go to Eton? You must know his arm should be healed first."

Her frigid tone gave him pause. He blinked, then he plunged into an obviously rehearsed speech. "My dear lady, it is my fondest wish that you will marry me. It would be no trouble at all for me to move in here for I know that you would find the vicarage far too small after the stately grandeur of Fairfax Hall. And I would be more than willing to assist you in managing the estate," he said triumphantly. It was obvious he believed his proposal all that a lady might wish. He opened his mouth as though to continue.

Claudia held up her hand to bring him to a halt. "Please, I beg of you, no more! I cannot marry you, sir."

"Cannot! But you have encouraged me for months!

I have been coming here, dining; we have had many comfortable chats . . ." He actually looked at a loss. Evidently it was beyond him to believe he could be rejected!

"Good day, vicar," said Hawke, sauntering into the drawing room. He glanced at the unlit hearth, then at Claudia. "Is it chilly in here, or is Edward's room rather warm?" To the stunned vicar he added, "I have been up assisting my ward with his splendid battle exhibit."

"It *is* somewhat chilly in here. I was about to suggest to Vicar Woodley that he leave." Claudia knew she was rude, but she was so angry she didn't trust herself not to blister the vicar's ears with a few of her thoughts on his presumptuousness.

"That would seem to be an excellent idea, my dear." Hawke strolled to her side, taking a position just behind her, placing his hand on the back of her chair perilously close to her shoulder. She could actually feel the heat of his body. She supposed he might appear to be rather possessive in his stance. For once, she would take advantage of his attitude and presence. If the vicar decided there was more to Lord Hawke's attention than actually existed, so be it.

"But . . ." sputtered the vicar as he looked from one to the other in appalled confusion.

Claudia daringly put her hand up so it rested on Hawke's. The vicar need not know that her display or her fatuous smile was a sham. "I know you will understand."

"Did you tell the vicar about Mrs. Alcock's cousin, my dear?" Hawke studied the befuddled man. "You *do* know that one of her cousins is a bishop, another is an earl? An influential gentleman from all I have heard. I should imagine a clever man would be all too willing to snap up Miss Alcock even if she didn't have a substantial dowry—which she does. More than substantial, if gossip has it correct. And gossip usually does with things of this sort." Hawke slowly caressed Claudia's other shoulder, an intimate gesture that was not missed by the vicar.

Vicar Woodley gaped a few moments, then hurriedly departed with a highly garbled excuse.

"Thank you, Lord Hawke," Claudia said, thankfully not sounding as shaken as she was. She rose, then shook her head. "That man! He wanted to marry me and move in here. Forgive me for acting as I did, but I thought it might lend weight to my refusal." She would not reveal how Hawke's caress of her shoulder affected her. "I had the feeling he intended to argue with me! To think I would permit that presumptuous puppy to move in here and take over the management of this estate . . . Well!"

"I have long suspected that to be the case. He is a fool, of course. He would not value you as you deserve." Hawke walked over to lightly touch her cheek. "You need a man who wants you for yourself and not for what you possess."

At that most interesting moment, Mrs. Tibbins came to the door, replenishment for the tea tray in hand. She glanced about in some puzzlement. "The vicar left?" Her face assumed a rather satisfied expression. "Pity, for I have more scones."

"Please, we will have our tea in the small sitting room. I find this room far too chilly." Claudia glanced at Hawke. "Will you join me, sir?"

"I do think you should consider your future, my dear," Hawke murmured as he ushered her into the cozy confines of the sitting room. "The vicar may not be to your liking, but surely you cannot continue as a widow. Such a shameful waste."

"With the sale of my land, I have sufficient money to purchase that pleasant house in Bath." She ignored his hint about her finding a second husband. There was only one man she desired, and she doubted he desired her as a wife. "Once Edward is off to Eton I shall think about removing to such a congenial place. Olivia can either remain here or . . ."

"Or wed Lodge. If I am any judge of matters, it will be Lodge. He shows all the symptoms of being top over tail in love with her. She will be doing very well for herself, you know."

"Indeed," Claudia said meekly, "I know he is heir to the Earl of Loxley. And I suspect that matters not a whit to Olivia. She would accept him were he to remain plain Mr. Lodge."

"Ears and all," Hawke added dryly.

"He was born that way and cannot help his looks. Olivia said she admires his mind. He is a prodigious thinker, according to her." Claudia sought refuge at the low table where Mrs. Tibbins now placed the tea set and the fresh scones. The vicar had managed to consume all of the first plate's contents prior to his unwelcome proposal.

"Blessings to Olivia, in that case. Now I should like my tea. Working with small boys is dry duty," he concluded in a plaintive note.

"Of course." She poured tea, passed scones, and attempted a lighthearted conversation. If Hawke was aware what a flutter her insides had become he had mercifully made no mention of it.

Sounds in the hallway indicated that someone had come. Several people, considering the noise.

Claudia glanced at Lord Hawke, then rose from her chair.

"I have such news," Olivia caroled as she breezed into the room, Mr. Lodge close behind her. "I shall travel with Mr. Lodge to meet his family. I am truly looking forward to it. Miss Cork will come along for propriety."

"Pace will go with us. The ladies can be inside the coach while Pace and I ride along. The family estate isn't all that far, perhaps two day's drive. And you may recall that Pace's place is close to mine."

"That is wonderful news," Claudia said, genuinely happy for Olivia. She would be mistress of her own home rather than a companion to her late cousin's widow.

James entered the room, beckoning Claudia aside. "Excuse me, ma'am. A woman has come from London with a box of gowns from Madame Clotilde. She says she's an assistant come to fit them on you in person."

Delighted with the prospect of a change in her dresses, Claudia went at once to instruct Mrs. Tibbins as to where the woman might stay. "I shall be up as soon as I am able. I am anxious to see what magic Madame has worked."

She returned to the small sitting room to find Hawke and Mr. Lodge deep in conversation. Olivia popped up to meet Claudia as she entered.

"You know what this means to me," she said softly. "Dearest of friends, I could only wish you will be as happy as I am."

"Thank you, dear Olivia." Seeing that the men showed no sign of ending their chat, she continued, "Would you like to see what came from London? Come with me."

They slipped from the room to rush up to where Claudia had requested the woman from London be housed. A gentle rap on the door brought the woman to greet them eagerly. It was clear she was more than pleased with her accommodations.

The huge box had been opened and several gowns were draped across the bed. A rich blue, a gorgeous green velvet, a pink kerseymere . . . and another gown, one of some magnificence.

"I did not order this," Claudia cried in dismay. Cream satin with lush peach roses begged to be tried on.

"I did," said Hawke from the doorway. "It will be useful."

Claudia gasped.

Chapter Sixteen

"*U*seful?" Claudia demanded in an awesomely quiet voice. She glanced at Madame Clotilde's assistant, then Olivia. Both women were wide-eyed, watching to see what happened next. After taking a deep breath, Claudia walked to where his lordship stood in the doorway, clasped one of his arms to lead him down the hall, and thrust him into a vacant bedroom. She followed, gently shutting the door behind her. Then she stared at him, allowing him to see how angry she had become.

"I do like the way you think, my dear. Bedrooms are among my favorite places to talk." He bestowed one of those bewitching smiles on her that normally would reduce her to a puddle of desire. Only the smile didn't affect her that way at the moment.

"*You* ordered a gown for me?" She pointed her index finger at him, then poked it at his chest. "Permit me to tell you that it simply isn't done, Lord Hawke. A gentleman does not go about giving a lady something as intimate as wearing apparel. Ever." She gave him a conscious look, adding, "Unless, of course, they are married."

"That does make it different." He gave her a sage nod.

"I also observed there is no bill with those gowns." She held out one slender hand, palm up. "I will pay my own bills, thank you very much. I will owe you nothing."

He smiled, lines crinkling up at the corners of his eyes in a beguiling manner. If she didn't know how alert he was, she would think his gaze sleepy. She knew better. This man was never less than awake on all suits—except when it came to her.

"I want you to have something pretty. Can't you simply accept it in the manner it is offered?" He took a firm hold on her finger, capturing her hand in his.

She fumed, trying to think of a suitable retaliation for his outrageous deed. "Apparently you do not consider me to be a lady, sir. I will have you know that I have behaved with all due propriety since my late husband went aloft. Olivia has been witness to my respectability." To her utter frustration she found tears in her eyes.

He saw them and looked dismayed, as well he might.

"I'll not have anyone saying I am not a fit mother for Edward." She sniffed, wondering why it was she never had a handkerchief when she wanted one.

Hawke pulled one from his pocket and dried off her tears.

"I'm sorry, Claudia." He shrugged. "I meant well. I know how limited your wardrobe is and that you longed for a few pretty gowns from London. Three gowns were not enough. Besides," and he gave her that wolfish grin again, "that gown would make a splendid wedding gown."

Her heart contracted in a spasm of pain. She refused to rise to what had to be his idea of teasing. She thought it tasteless, to say the least. "I will not dignify that last bit with a reply." She spoiled her attempt to be haughty with the need to blow her nose.

"Please keep the gown. It is a mere trifle, and I would see you wear it. You will be all peaches and cream in it." Those blue eyes saw far too much. He *knew* she had fallen in love with that gown the moment she spotted it.

Drat the man! However, the gown was gorgeous and she couldn't bear to return it to London. "I will keep it *if* you will give me the bill."

"Very well," he said far too meekly. "I must have a record of it somewhere. Might take a bit of time to find it."

With that she had to be content. She knew she had better get out of the bedroom before the wretched man thought of the various ways and means to be entertained therein. She had an idea that he knew far too much about things like that.

Returning to the room where the assistant waited with Olivia, Claudia said nothing more in respect to the cream satin gown, other than to request that it be fitted.

Olivia breathed a sigh of relief. "I am so glad you will not return it." She fingered the rich satin, touched one of the peach silk roses. "You know, this gown would make a perfectly wonderful wedding gown. I can see it now."

"Well, don't. In order for it to be a wedding gown I have to have a groom and I do not possess such a thing." She conveniently ignored the vicar's proposal. She would remain a widow the rest of her life before marrying him.

"I think . . ." Olivia began before Claudia cut her off.

"What will you take along to meet Mr. Lodge's family? I vow it is far more exciting than my getting a few gowns from London. And Dorothy Cox will go with you? How lovely to have a friend at your side. You will be so much more comfortable that way." The attempt to change Olivia's thoughts worked, and Claudia had to listen to her happy chatter while the assistant checked the fit of the several gowns.

Later, over dinner, Claudia offered her best wishes

not only for the journey, but also for their future. It was clear that both Olivia and Dorothy would have excellent prospects with men they dearly loved.

"It will seem strange not to see you and dear little Edward," Olivia said with a watery voice.

"We will visit you. Besides, Edward will be going off to Eton one of these days, and I may take up residence in Bath." This bit of news brought forth a flurry of questions and the tears Claudia had feared were averted.

The foursome left on the next day. Madam Clotilde's assistant left the day after that, as there was little to be done on the gowns.

The house was frightfully quiet. Edward was subdued. Not even Hawke came over from his home. Claudia hated to admit it, but she missed the miserable man. He certainly was entertaining, if nothing else.

She concentrated on painting her porcelain. Edward admired his plate, wondering when he would he able to use it.

"Mr. Fry has ordered a new kiln to be built for me. I am not satisfied with the old one. You will see then, it will be splendid." She patted his shoulder in affection before returning to her enamel work.

With that, Edward had to be satisfied. He spent hours in the nursery where his battlefield had been set up, arranging the soldiers and cannon around the village Lord Hawke had brought him. His arm slowly healed and Jem Groom continued to allow the boy to sit on Humbug, walking about at a sedate pace.

The fairies were being most cooperative, peeping up from behind the various flowers. Perhaps she might be the only one to see them, but she thought them charming and to capture them on porcelain seemed very right, somehow. She drew fairies garbed in the latest styles from *La Belle Assemblée* waving delicate wands and having the most graceful of poses. What Lord Hawke might think of these latest efforts she couldn't imagine. He had said he wanted to view her little fairies. That was most likely polite talk, nothing more. He had not evinced further interest.

When she grew tired of her painting, Claudia wandered about in the enclosed garden, thinking about Lord Hawke. Was he done with her? She had heard nothing about a new woman in his life. Her maid was quick to pass along news from Hawke's Rest. According to her gossip, his lordship was getting the house and land as fine as five pence, quite as though he intended going away. Perhaps he was tired of rustication? There were none of the pleasures of London found around here. Of course, from all she'd heard, London was quiet this time of year as far as *ton* pastimes were concerned. With Society off to the country for shooting and hunting, amusements were thin on the ground.

"So what," she wondered aloud in the peace of her little painting room, "was the man plotting?"

By the end of that first week she had almost finished the set of twelve plates. It was early in the morning when James showed him into the painting room. Startled, Claudia dropped her brush. It had been loaded with blue enamel and splattered on the table, fortunately *not* on the porcelain.

"I surprised you. I am sorry, my dear. How does the painting go on?" He strolled across the room to study the results of many hours of labor now resting on the special racks Claudia had ordered made.

"As you see. And you?" she dared inquire. "I trust all is well with you and your house?"

"As you see. That is, I am in fine fettle. When do I see your fairies?" he demanded, albeit nicely.

"Any dawn will do," she replied, suppressing a grin at the thought of the elegant Lord Hawke, the pride of London drawing rooms and balls, deigning to rise before dawn in order to see a fairy. If, that is, the fairies would cooperate. So far, Claudia had been the only one to see them and not all that often. It was odd how popular fairies were at the present. Olivia had suggested that the china factories might be interested in obtaining the fairy plate designs to produce for others who loved fairies. Dorothy Cork thought the designs would be splendid put in a book. Fond mamas would buy the books for their offspring.

Claudia had decided to keep the drawings private, just for her own pleasure. She glanced at the results of her efforts. "Mr. Fry has ordered plans for a new kiln. The workmen will construct it as soon as the plans arrive. I am very anxious."

"So am I, actually." He slowly paced about the room, pausing now and again to examine one of the plates waiting to be fired. The enamel had dried, but needed high heat to finish the process.

"I can see why I should be eager. Why should you care one way or the other?" She gave him a puzzled look.

"I have plans that involve you. Until you are through with this painting business, I must wait," he explained after some pause while he deliberated. Apparently she wasn't to know what those plans included.

"But you still wish to see the fairies?"

"I do."

Such a solemn agreement surprised her. He might almost be making a vow! He picked up a plate to examine it.

"It takes a great amount of heat, does it not?"

"True. My old kiln couldn't seem to get hot enough to produce a proper firing. Half-baked can apply to china as well as other items." She gave him a impish look.

"The new kiln will be safe?"

"I believe so. I know there is a small risk involved, but I have not had a problem to date."

"But your old kiln wasn't heating properly. The new

will generate far more heat. I would not like to think of you as being in danger." He gave her a concerned look.

"Oh, pooh. Now you sound like Olivia."

"Have you heard from Miss Greene and Miss Cork? Pace dropped me a line to say his parents found Miss Cork exemplary, and not merely for her dowry and connections. Lodge introduced Miss Greene to the earl. I gather it was a momentous meeting. I had no idea that Miss Greene possessed so much backbone."

"She once told me you are a dangerous man."

He stopped and tilted his head to study Claudia, a frown creasing his brow. "No. No one could consider me dangerous!"

"You managed to turn my life upside down," she admitted.

"Edward is to leave for Eton shortly. Mr. Beemish said his arm has healed admirably. You will miss him, yet you must know it is for his good." Thankfully, he ignored her confession.

Claudia rose and walked to look out of the window. "I am reconciled to his going. He hates to leave Humbug behind. I promised him the pony would be awaiting his holidays."

"One by one things are falling into place," Hawke murmured. He didn't explain that odd remark, which left Claudia all the more wondering what was in his mind.

Mr. Fry paused at the doorway, then entered with a packet in hand. "The plans have come, and I shall put the bricklayers to work as soon as may be."

"High-temperature firebrick, I assume," Hawke inserted.

"Naturally. I have been in touch with the gentleman who supplies the porcelain for Lady Fairfax. I am following his suggestions for the new kiln. It should be quite splendid."

They conversed for a time before Mr. Fry returned to his paperwork.

"Walk with me to the stables." Hawke held out a hand to Claudia.

She placed hers in his, thinking of what Adela had said about trust. Indeed, it was as she had said: Trust was relying on someone. And her hopes? Her yearning, longing for a future that might never become reality? She couldn't know. In the interim, she had Hawke at her side, and she would not ask for more at the moment—even if that wee voice at the back of her mind insisted a kiss or more would be very welcome.

They paused before the stable door. "I will be here before dawn in the morning. Must I wake you?" His grin told her that was something he might enjoy doing—wicked man.

"I will be up. I often rise early so it is no problem for me." She supposed her skepticism showed, for he gave her that marvelous slow smile that lit his eyes.

"I promise you that if you are not awaiting me at the garden gate I will gladly do the necessary. Cold water?"

"Hawke!" she cried, unable to prevent a laugh. "You are incorrigible."

"Perhaps I am," he agreed to her confusion.

He left her then, striding over to where Kismet waited for him. Claudia watched until he was but a puff of dust in the distance.

Hawke reached his home without incident. He walked into the house deeply in thought. Was he doing the right thing? He was in love with Claudia Fairfax. He believed she loved him in return. But the lady had been childless in her marriage to a man who had fathered five children. Could Hawke deal with that? The matter vexed him no end, for he had found no answer. Could love overcome the obstacle of a childless marriage when an heir was so desirable? Yet, if he wed a virgin, there was no guarantee.

The coming days would tell him the truth of the matter, perhaps. And then perhaps not. He would have to trust all would be well.

The dawn chorus of birds had begun when Claudia slipped from her bed. She dressed quickly, tossing a warm shawl around her shoulders before slipping down to the kitchen. Cook had banked the fire and it took but a slight stirring before the coals burst forth in a small flame—enough to heat a bit of water for tea. With cup in hand and a crust of bread, she left the house for the garden gate.

Standing by the weathered wood, she thought back to the first time he had met her here. He had kissed her, a punishing kiss as though it was her fault that he found her . . . what? Appealing? Handy? Available? The sound of a horse on the avenue's gravel brought her head around in time to see Hawke approaching. A slow smile curved her lips.

"You are too late to wake me, Hawke," she said quietly, with consideration for all the servants who might be asleep. Never mind they would soon be stirring.

"Drat! I looked forward to rousing you, my dear." He quickly joined her by the gate. Looking it over, he returned his gaze to her face. "Do you remember our meeting here? I have rather fond memories of that occasion."

"You kissed me and *I* neglected to slap that arrogant face," she whispered. His expression amused her.

"I ought to refresh those memories, I think." With no more warning, he gathered her close to him and placed a warm kiss on her lips. He ignored her raised hand, tucking it next to him.

"Better, but there is room for improvement, I believe."

She flashed him a look for his impudence, then opened the gate to enter into the pretty garden where her fairies might be found. Sometimes. If they were in the mood to appear, that is.

"I cannot promise anything, you know. As far as I am aware, they have appeared for no one else save me." She spoke with a soft, low voice. She had talked to the fairies, but they had never spoken to her. Likely she wouldn't understand their language if they did.

She motioned him to stand quite still, and they waited for a time. She was about to give up when a tiny figure peeped around the fuchsia plant. Another peeked over the vast hydrangea bloom. Nudging Hawke, she nodded toward the flowers in question.

"Well, I'll be," he whispered. "I thought you teasing me." He looked utterly flabbergasted.

She fastened her gaze on the two tiny figures. "I have painted both of these ladies. They are so beautiful."

Apparently the lady fairies understood, for they looked quite pleased. One pirouetted around atop a fuchsia bloom, while the other waved her wand. She had a star in her hair and her wings were sheerest gauze. All of a sudden, a dragonfly swooped down and allowed the fairy to mount his back. Within seconds the pair had flown off.

Claudia glanced at Hawke, who wore a look of utter disbelief. Well, it was scarcely your everyday sight.

The other fairy stretched out on a fuchsia leaf, seeming ready for a nap. The leaf obligingly curled up around her and she was lost to view.

"We may as well leave now. I doubt any others will appear."

They closed the garden gate behind them in silence.

"Thank you for sharing that with me," Hawke said when they neared the house. "It is incredible—like stepping into another world." He paused, listening to the sounds of the house waking up and the servants preparing for another day.

"Before I leave . . ."

"Yes?"

"I said there was room for improvement. Perhaps we might try again?" He didn't wait for an answer but took her into his arms. Alas, the kiss was not to be—to Claudia's disappointment. Jem Groom came out of the stables, caught sight of Kismet tethered to a post, and looked around.

"I will see you later."

It sounded to Claudia's ears as though he made a promise. Things too good to be true usually were.

The bricklayers worked steadily at their task, with the neat little kiln rising almost before her eyes. She checked on it often, which most likely spurred the men on with their task.

By the following day all was accomplished. It took time for the brick to cure sufficiently for the kiln to be tested.

Claudia took a small plate to make a trial. She wanted to be certain that the kiln was indeed safe for her precious porcelain.

The fire, built and maintained until it reached a maximum temperature, gave off more heat then she anticipated.

"I would have thought that the design would have kept more heat inside," she commented to Mr. Fry as they studied the structure.

Satisfied that the heat was as high as it might reach, she opened the door, placed the plate on a rack with a special tool she had used in the past, then shut the door with care.

Mr. Fry returned to his office, satisfied the new design was all that had been promised. Claudia remained for a while, wondering how well the kiln would work.

She had stepped away with the thought of spending some time in her garden when it happened. The kiln blew up!

The explosion rocked the area, sending shards of hot brick and fire in all directions. She had moved far enough away so she escaped the worst of the blast, but her skin burned wherever she had been pelted with the fragments. She felt on fire.

Clothing offered little protection against the incredibly high temperatures that had been reached. Her screams brought servants rushing to her side. Jem Groom brought a pail of water to douse the flames. Mrs. Tibbins followed, anxious to help.

Some of the water splashed on Claudia. It was icy cold and all she could think of was to plunge into a tub of cold water to ease the pain of the little burns that covered the front of her body.

When Hawke heard of the blast, he dashed to Fairfax Hall and his darling Claudia with all speed. Brushing aside Mrs. Tibbins and James, he tore up the stairs and into the room he knew was Claudia's. Mrs. Tibbins's words of protest followed him.

His little love reclined on her bed covered with a sheet. Her garments were a pile of tattered cloth. Pain etched her chalk white face. "I'm not in very fine fettle at the moment."

"Claudia, my dearest." Hawke gazed at his love, his heart constricted, and his fears soared. He knew she was in pain, but how serious the burns might be he couldn't guess.

"You ought not be here," she murmured just loud enough for him to hear, "but I am glad to see you."

Hawke gingerly picked up one hand, noting as he did that the back of it bore a small burn. Carefully turning it over, he placed a gentle kiss on her palm. "This is my worst nightmare," he said, his voice tight with feeling. "I will not leave you, my dear." He pulled up a chair and perched by the bed.

"The burns are not terribly serious. I know I will be much better tomorrow. Mrs. Tibbins will use her special ointment. She has summoned Mr. Beemish as well."

"They will ease your pain. You will be better in no time."

Claudia appeared to relax at his comforting words. Hawke vowed to remain as long as permitted. The shock of seeing the one he loved brought so low convinced him that his love for Claudia went far beyond the need for an heir. He loved her because of what she was, her inner qualities, and not merely her beauty. Even were she to be scarred, he would love her no less. A future with her was all he asked. What did an heir matter if it deprived him of the woman he loved?

Mrs. Tibbins quietly brought in a basin of some herbal solution and began to sponge the burns, beginning with Claudia's arms. "You must go." She looked at Hawke with mild reproach.

"No. I will help. She is to be my wife. There is no reason I shall be barred from her side." His firm reply brought a knowing smile from the housekeeper.

Hawke scarcely left the room all that day. Only when Mrs. Tibbins insisted that Claudia needed personal care was he ousted. In the hall he found a frightened little boy.

Edward cried onto Hawke's shoulder, afraid he would lose his mama. But Claudia was resilient. By the next day she had responded to the tender ministrations of those who cared for her. Within a few days she was sitting up, wincing at the stiff skin on her burns, but finding a shard of humor in the disaster.

"At least Edward's dragon plate wasn't in there. Thank you, Hawke, for all you have done. I think you must eat and sleep a little. You are not your polished self." Her gaze caressed him, and her eyes held her deepest love in them.

He went home then, relieved her burns responded to the ointment, and there would be no serious scars. While he could overlook them, he suspected she could not.

At the end of the week he found her in her sitting room with a pot of tea and a book. She set it aside when he entered. He took heart at her loving smile. There was no doubt of her welcome.

"I suppose you may guess why I have come." Dressed in his very best afternoon garb for the occasion, he hoped she might.

Her chin tilted up and her smile was flirtatious. "I cannot guess, my dear." Her eyes promised much.

"I beg you to marry me. Dearest Claudia, I promise to love and care for you the rest of my life." He kissed her, gently for fear he might hurt her.

"I will gladly marry you, my love. I will honor, love, and care for you all of my life as well." Which called for another kiss.

Hawke produced a special license from an inside pocket where he had placed it earlier. He waved it before a bemused Claudia. He lightly touched her chin with one gentle finger. "I fell in love with you when I first saw you at your marriage to my friend and neighbor, Basil Fairfax. I buried my love, thinking it pointless to pursue so chaste and proper a young wife. But you were always in my heart. Always." This declaration was reason for a most satisfying kiss, one that promised much.

"And now we can be together forever," Claudia said, smiling with utter bliss. She ignored the remains of her aches to snuggle closer in his arms. Indeed, to her mind, heaven could not be any better, even if her papa said otherwise.

The entire village—from Mrs. Alcock, her husband and daughter to the other inhabitants of the area— attended the modish wedding at the village church.

The newly engaged vicar, having taken the plunge and asked Mary Alcock to wed, shared honors with Mr. Herbert. The rector was polite, but scarcely more than that, to the vicar's disappointment. After all, the eminent Mr. Herbert was highly regarded in church circles and very well connected to some of the highest families.

A radiant Claudia, Lady Fairfax became the beloved bride of Noel, Viscount Hawke. The former baroness accepted the position of viscountess with every evidence of great happiness. Dressed in cream satin trimmed with peach silk roses, she was an incomparable. Her groom, resplendent in his best, matched her for elegance.

No one saw the tiny creatures lurking in the arrangement of the flowers in the church other than the bride and her groom.

Lord Elliot, along with his wife Adela, had traveled from London for the occasion. Olivia joined in the festivities, secure her day would come soon.

Mrs. Herbert gazed with contentment as her eldest married a man she obviously loved with all her generous heart.

Epilogue

June 1818

"*H*e is a handsome infant, is he not?" Claudia cooed at her firstborn son, with a side-glance at her terribly proud and excessively handsome husband.

"The best, but I fancy we are a trifle partial." Noel bent over to touch the satiny cheek of his precious heir. "What a lot of infants there are in your family, my love. I am truly amazed that your sisters all brought their offspring along to Harry's baptism. We have a veritable nursery here!"

"It was an opportunity for us all to visit and show off our babies. We were close as sisters. I can only hope our children will be as close." Claudia tickled the cheek of her baby, thankful for the blessing of a son to her wonderful marriage. She had feared she would be unable to give her husband an heir, what with all the childless years while married to Basil. True, he had not sought her bed often, charmed by Mrs. Norton. Thus, she was more than delighted at her precious child.

"Tell me, twins do not run in your family, do they? Tabitha says she is expecting twins. I must say I am not the slightest surprised, given her girth." Noel grinned at his affronted wife even as he looked a bit apprehensive.

"Noel!" Claudia laughed. "To set you at ease, they run in Hugh's family." Her face became reflective. "It is so marvelous. Nympha has a fine boy and Nick looks proud as a peacock. Priscilla's little girl is adorable and I must say that Felix looks as though he would welcome a half dozen like her. Adrian is obviously proud of his heir. 'Tis obvious Drusilla dotes on both of her men—young and old."

"You must feel rather smug, matchmaking as you have. Who would have thought that when Elliot, Pace, and Lodge—now Loxley—came to visit they would end up married to your friends?"

"Olivia is so right for Lord Loxley. She makes a splendid countess. And you must admit that Dorothy is well matched with Lord Pace. They will likely have a clutch of horse-mad children. I suspect Max lost his heart to Adela the day they met. I know that she felt an instant attraction to him."

Noel nodded, feeling a trifle smug as well. "Your brother and Emma are settling in nicely. She became rather ill on the trip here. She doesn't *look* like one of those sickly females."

"Pregnancy will do that, you know. I can scarce believe that Adam received a barony. Great-uncle Stanwell managed it. Who would have thought he would exert himself for so distant a relative?"

"You have an exceptional family, my love. I must say, I do enjoy all my new relatives." He eased down beside her. "Especially you." They embarked on a most delightful kiss that could easily lead to something more interesting.

A tap on the door brought a halt to this activity. It was time to join the others.

Gathering her infant in her arms, Claudia and her dearly beloved husband left the nursery for the ride to the church where her father would baptize his latest grandchild.

Once all were settled in the pews, it could be noted

that the Herbert family had done amazingly well for themselves. At least, Mrs. Herbert thought so as she surveyed her flock. She sent up a brief, though heart-felt, prayer of thanks for her many and rather noisy blessings.

Fairies in the Regency Period

Shakespeare introduced a literary fairyland in *The Tempest* and *A Midsummer Night's Dream* that inspired any number of artists to paint and poets to write about the world of fairies. Shelley in his *Hymn of Pan* and in *Wine of the Fairies,* Ben Jonson in *Gipsy Song,* John Milton in *Arcades,* all extol a fairy world. Thomas Hood in *Queen Mab* wrote:

> *A little fairy comes at night,*
> *Her eyes are blue, her hair is brown,*
> *With silver spots upon her wings,*
> *And from the moon she flutters down.*

Margaret Cavendish, Duchess of Newcastle, penned a delightful poem of a fairy queen and Amelia Jane Murray painted a series of watercolors that featured delicate fairies garbed in Regency dress in a fragile fairy world.

Actually, people have looked for signs of fairies on propitious nights such as Midsummer's Eve for centuries. The painted fairies were often beautiful and kind, and stories revealed their shyness with humans. There was the mischief maker Puck, or Robin Goodfellow, who performed all manner of tricks on humans. Other fairies were cunning and sly, quick to play humans for fools. Literature and art dealing with fairies were popular in the Regency period.

Having a heroine see and paint delicate fairies peeping over flowers and mingling with butterflies and dragonflies is quite fitting.

Emily Hendrickson

The Madcap Heiress

Adam Herbert yearns
for adventure.
What he finds is heiress
Emily Lawrence.
Together they discover a
love worth more than
any fortune.

0-451-21289-4

Signet

REGENCY ROMANCE
NOW AVAILABLE

Diamond Dreams
by Sandra Heath

An impulsive kiss between a down-on-her-luck woman
and a mysterious stranger leads to adventure—and
passion—in exotic St. Petersburg.

0-451-21449-8

Lady Larkspur Declines
by Sharon Sobel

Desperate to avoid an arranged—and loveless—
marriage, Lady Larkspur fakes an illness only to fall
victim to her handsome doctor's bedside manner.

0-451-21459-5

Available wherever books are sold or at
www.penguin.com